THE STRANGER'S WIFE

HILDA STAHL

Other books available
in this Prairie Series:

BLOSSOMING LOVE

THE MAKESHIFT HUSBAND

Published by
Bethel Publishing Company
1819 South Main Street
Elkhart, Indiana 46516

Cover Illustration by Ed French
Edited by Grace Pettifor

Printed in the United States of America

ISBN 0-934998-44-2

DEDICATED WITH LOVE
TO BROCK & BODIE THOENE
You touched my life
in a special way
Thanks

CHAPTER 1

A shiver ran down Maple's spine. This was 1890, not the dark ages! And she was twenty-five years old, not a child! Why didn't she have the courage to stand up to Momma and jerk off the wedding gown, run out of the church, and gallop her horse across the Nebraska sandhills to freedom? The scent of roses in her bouquet sickened her. At the sound of the organ playing the Wedding March she hung back, but Momma forced her through the door of the coatroom to the tiny foyer where Papa stood waiting for her. A gust of hot June wind rattled the outside door.

"Don't you dare dash down the aisle with her, Mr. Raines!" Leona Raines whispered, her dark eyes flashing.

Maple's jaw tightened, but she couldn't speak up to Momma. She'd never been able to stand against Momma's sharp tongue.

"I won't, Mrs. Raines." Ben Raines took Maple's arm and his lean face softened into a smile. Laugh lines spread from the corners of his blue eyes to his graying red hair. He was taller and leaner than she was. His black suit fit him well, but looked strange on him. He usually wore heavy denim pants and shirt, a white Stetson hat, and slanted high-heeled boots. She saw the love for her in his eyes. Maybe if she begged hard enough, he'd let her run away. "Ready, my girl?"

"Of course she's ready," Leona snapped as she straightened her dark blue hat and patted her thick waist. She closed her eyes, took a deep breath, and walked through the double doors into the sanctuary, leaving a trail of lavender scent behind.

Maple leaned against Papa and looked into his face. They had the same long nose with the slight hump, high, flat cheek-bones, and almost gaunt figures. "Don't make me do this!" Her voice came out in a hoarse whisper. "Let me ride back to the ranch and hide from Momma."

Ben shook his head. "No, Maple girl. This is better for you. I won't always be around to take care of you. Mr. Turner will make you a fine husband."

Maple flushed painfully. She'd heard often enough that she was too tall and too thin to be beautiful and that men didn't want a woman who could ride a horse and brand a calf and swing a rope like the cowboys on Papa's ranch. A man wanted a gentle, soft woman to fix meals, tend the children, and share his bed.

"Do me proud today, daughter. Walk down that aisle with your head up and your back straight. Be a good wife to Mr. Turner." Ben rubbed his rough hand over Maple's. "You'll be your own woman as Mrs. Ed Turner. I give you my word I'll keep your

momma out of your affairs." Ben looked through
the veil deep into Maple's blue eyes. "Will you
walk tall, Maple?"

She hesitated, then nodded. "I'll do it for you,
Papa."

"I knew you would."

She bit her lip to hold back the cry of anguish.

The Wedding March swelled and Ben pushed
open the double doors. Edward Turner and Pastor
VanArsdale stood at the altar of the only church in
Keene. They both looked nervous. The church held
about fifty people and it was almost full. Ben Raines
was an important rancher. From the wooden pews
the guests turned to stare at Maple. Were they
thinking how ugly she was or how lucky she was
to be marrying the only banker in Keene? The afternoon sunlight streaming through the long window
at the side of the church gleamed off the bald spot
on Mr. Turner's dark head. His round face turned red
as he watched her walk toward him. He was a head
shorter than she was and, at forty years, almost as
wide as he was tall. He pressed his palms against his
round legs as he stepped out to meet her. She
trembled and the color drained from her face, making her strawberry blonde hair look brighter red.

Ben squeezed her hand, then handed her over to
Mr. Turner. Together they faced the pastor. The
music stopped and the room seemed deathly silent.
Maple's mouth turned bone dry. She smelled Mr.
Turner's hair oil and felt the heat of his body.

Pastor VanArsdale cleared his throat. He was of
medium build with gray hair and watery blue eyes.

"We are gathered together this afternoon in the sight of God to unite in holy matrimony this man and this woman."

Suddenly the foyer doors banged open. Maple jumped and turned to see who had caused the disturbance. She gasped and the church buzzed with whispers as five men strode in dressed in dusty, rough garb, their guns slung low and tied around their legs. Maple gripped her bouquet tighter.

"What's the meaning of this, Brindle?" Ed Turner snapped, his face brick-red.

Brindle pushed his sweat-stained gray hat to the back of his head and grinned, showing tobacco-stained, decayed teeth. He was tall and thin with a stubby beard, dirty, dark hair almost hidden by an old hat with a drooping brim, and dark eyes as hard as coal. "Buck Lincoln sent me to town to fetch you, Turner. He has bankin' business he wants tended today."

Maple's heart leaped. Maybe this was her way out! Buck Lincoln was the biggest rancher in the Nebraska sandhills and he always got his way. She darted a look at Papa. His face was dark with anger. Momma held his arm tightly to keep him from attacking Brindle. Maple willed Papa to stay in his seat.

Ed tugged impatiently at his jacket. "Mr. Lincoln will have to wait. I'm getting married. Sit down or leave, but don't disturb me." Ed turned around and pulled Maple back in place. "Proceed, Pastor."

Brindle growled low in his throat and pushed

his way between Ed and Maple. "Buck Lincoln ain't in the habit of waitin' for nothin', not even a weddin'!" He jerked his head and his men drew their guns and crowded around Ed and Maple.

As the guests gasped Maple ducked her head to hide the light in her eyes. She knew she should be frightened. If anyone moved, they might be shot without a second thought. Buck Lincoln's men were known for their meanness.

Brindle gripped Ed's arm and hauled him close. "You're comin' with me."

Ed shook his head stubbornly. "Tell Lincoln I'll see him before we go on our honeymoon since it's that important."

"He said now!"

"I am getting married! Get out and take your men with you!"

A shiver ran down Maple's spine. It was dangerous to defy Brindle. She hadn't realized Mr. Turner was so brave.

Ben pulled away from Leona and reared up. "Get out of this church now!"

Brindle spun around and aimed his Colt right at Ben's heart. "Sit down!"

Leona cried out and jerked Ben down.

Maple bit her lip, her heart hammering as she willed Papa to keep silent.

Pastor cleared his throat. "Please be seated and let us proceed. The ceremony is short."

Ed shook his head. "I won't let you continue until these men are out of the church." He glared at Brindle. "Now get out or there won't be a wedding and I won't meet with Mr. Lincoln!"

Brindle eyed Ed, then laughed wickedly. "You're awful big for your breeches, ain't you?"

Maple's stomach tightened. What was Brindle going to do?

Brindle gripped Ed's arm and shoved him at two of his men. "Take him to his buggy and see that he gets to Buck."

The men hauled Ed Turner out, kicking and shouting. Maple's pulse leaped. She was free!

Chuckling, Brindle turned back to the pastor. "I'm in the mood to see a weddin'." Brindle studied his two remaining men. "Montana, get over here and marry this red-haired lady."

His face pale, Montana shook his shaggy head. "Not me, boss. I ain't the marryin' kind. Let Banty marry her. He has a soft spot for strawberry blonde hair."

Maple's head swam and she almost fell. She heard Momma gasp.

"You won't get by with this!" Ben growled.

Brindle cocked his Colt. "You objectin'?"

"No!" Leona cried, shaking her head as she clung to Ben.

Brindle chuckled and eased the hammer down. "Get over here, Banty!"

Banty laughed and slapped his skinny leg. Dust rose around him. "I would, boss, but I got me a wife down in Texas. You marry her."

Brindle snaked a long arm around Maple's narrow waist and grinned down into her ashen face. "That might be fun, but I don't reckon I want me a bride."

Maple trembled.

Brindle turned back to his men. "We're gonna have us some fun here. I saw Hadley Clements in town. Montana, you get outside and you find that tall scarecrow and bring him here. He'll be the groom. Lincoln will get a kick out of that."

"I can't allow that!" Pastor VanArsdale said.

"Shut up!"

Maple swayed and would have fallen but Brindle tightened his arm.

"Don't faint on me now, woman! You're gonna have yourself a real weddin' with a scarecrow."

Maple helplessly shook her head. Who was this man they were going to force her to marry? She glanced at the pastor. His rugged face was wet with sweat and his eyes wide with fear. She looked over her shoulder at her parents. She knew they couldn't help her.

A few minutes later the door burst open and Montana pushed in a tall, thin man with shaggy hair and beard. Blood trickled down the side of his face and down his right arm. His hat was gone and his long dark hair was matted with sweat and dirt. His boots scraped loudly against the plank floor.

"Clements, you're a sight for sore eyes!" Brindle slapped Hadley on the shoulder and laughed. "This is your lucky day." Brindle pushed Hadley up beside Maple. "Get 'em married, parson!"

Hadley frowned. Was this a nightmare or was it really happening? He had come to town for supplies, the first time in six months, and was driving out of town when Montana had shot at him and yelled for him to stop. The bullet had grazed his arm and knocked him off the wagon. Before he could move, Montana had struck his head with his gun barrel. Now his head ached and his right arm burned. He'd had enough of Brindle's meanness this past year. "Stop this foolishness right now, Brindle!" Hadley's voice was crisp with anger.

Brindle narrowed his eyes. "You want me to shoot this lady down where she stands?"

Hadley glanced at the woman. She looked ready to pass out. He couldn't take a chance on Brindle shooting her. Hadley slowly shook his head.

Maple shivered and the bouquet fell from her lifeless fingers. Banty scooped it up and pushed it into her arms. She clung to it helplessly. They were actually going to force her to marry this stranger!

Pastor VanArsdale cleared his throat. "I . . . really must object to . . . this!"

"Object away and then get on with it." Brindle pointed the blue barrel of his Colt right in the pastor's face.

Maple lifted her eyes again to the tall man beside her and he nodded his head slightly. He reached for her hand. With a strangled moan she held her hand out to him. His fingers closed over hers. He squeezed her hand as if to reassure her. The room whirled, then steadied as the pastor hoarsely read through the ceremony making them husband and wife.

Chuckling, Brindle prodded Hadley in the ribs. "Kiss yer bride!"

Maple gasped as she stared in horror at her groom.

His heart jerked. He'd never kissed a woman before—aside from his ma and sisters. His hands steady, he awkwardly lifted her veil.

"No," she whispered. She smelled his sweat and dirt.

He gripped her arms and pulled her closer, then lowered his face and kissed her lips in a hard, firm kiss. He released her and turned away, unable to look at her in his embarrassment.

Her mouth tingled. Not even Mr. Turner had kissed her on the lips before. She scrubbed at her mouth with the back of her hand. She rubbed her cheeks to try to erase the feel of his whiskers.

Brindle and his men shouted with laughter. Brindle pointed his Colt into the air and fired. The blast filled the room and left a hole in the ceiling. "Take yer bride to yer wagon."

Hadley wanted to refuse, but he knew the danger.

Helplessly, Maple looked up at the stranger, then back at her parents. Momma was crying hysterically and Papa's face was black with rage.

Hadley's fingers bit into Maple's arm through the satin sleeve as they stepped outdoors where wind whipped her veil and dress. Last winter's tumbleweed blew across the churchyard and off into the prairie. She looked for help down the street toward the general store and the bank, but the street was deserted. He led her to the wagon beside the hitching post at the side of the church. A tarp covered the supplies in the back. The bay mares hitched to the wagon moved restlessly. A dog barked at the side of the sod schoolhouse across the dusty street.

"Get up there!" Brindle prodded Hadley in the back with his gun barrel.

Hadley hesitated, then sprang up and settled on the high wooden seat. Sweat soaked him as he sought for a plan of escape. Silently he cried out for God to help him.

Shivering, Maple hung back, shaking her head. "I won't go with him!"

The men swore at her and lifted her to the seat. The mares nickered and bobbed their heads. Maple fell against Hadley and quickly moved away from him. Her veil swung forward and hid her pale face. The hot sun burned down on her.

Hadley gathered the reins in his bony hands. "Hang on, miss," he whispered gruffly. Maybe he could outrun the men.

Maple darted a look at him, then braced her feet and clung to the seat.

Hadley slapped the reins against the bays and shouted. The team leaped ahead and the wagon jerked forward. Brindle yelled and shot. Dust rose up around them and settled on Maple's white wedding gown, turning it gray. She looked back over her shoulder. Brindle, Montana, and Banty were riding hard after them, yelling and shooting into the air. With a moan she turned back around, holding on for dear life as the wagon bounced and swayed. A gust of wind whipped her veil over on Hadley. She flushed and yanked it off her head. She flung it over the side of the wagon for the horses to trample until it looked like a saddlebum's old bandanna. She gripped the rough seat again. Strands of red hair tumbled around her shoulders and cascaded down her back. Would the men shoot them or get tired of the chase and leave them alone? Surely Papa would rescue her before anything terrible happened to her.

Just then a cloud covered the sun and the sky darkened. In the distance thunder rumbled.

"A storm might help us, miss." Hadley looked straight ahead as he shouted over the creak of the wagon.

"A gun would help!" She scowled angrily at him. "Where's yours?"

"They took 'em!" His head felt as if it would explode. His right arm burned and he felt the strength draining out of it. Would the men give up the chase and leave them be? He couldn't keep the team under control much longer.

"Why didn't you stop them?"

"I tried!"

"Why didn't you refuse to marry me?"

He glanced at her. "I saw that pretty red hair and couldn't help myself."

She flushed scarlet. How could he tease her at a time like this? "We won't be married for long! Papa will rescue me and the minister will write off the wedding." The wind snatched her words away. Dust billowed around them as the horses raced across the barely visible trail through the prairie grass. Lightning zigzagged across the vast sky. Thunder boomed and Maple jumped. Was it only a thunderstorm or would rain fall soon? Maple glanced back over her shoulder. Brindle was laughing. He was staying behind them, knowing they couldn't stop or turn back as long as he was there.

Just then the wagon wheel hit a deep rut. The pull on the reins shot sharp pains through Hadley's arm. The jangle of harness faded and he knew he was blacking out. He thrust the reins at Maple.

Surprised, she grabbed the reins. She saw him sway. What was wrong with him? Alarmed, she grabbed his arm and jerked him back in place.

His head spun, but he managed to hold himself erect.

"What's wrong with you?" she shouted.

"I been shot."

"Shot?" Her heart sank. Suddenly a great drop of rain plopped on her cheek. Frantically she looked up at the sky. The thunderclouds were closer and darker. She glanced back. Brindle and his men were looking up at the sky, not making an effort to catch them. Just what were they up to? She turned back. "Where are we going?" she shouted.

"To my place," he managed to answer.

"How much further?"

"Another hour."

She shot a look at him. "Can you make it?"

He nodded grimly. He could do anything he had to. Without the pull of the reins he could tolerate the pain in his arm and head.

"Tell me where to go."

"Follow the trail until you reach that hill with the blow-out." He pointed to a tall hill with the side of it cut away by the wind, revealing the sand beneath. "Head west across the prairie to my place."

She wanted to ask what he thought Brindle was going to do with them, but it was too hard to hear over the noise.

The sun burned down on her and she longed for her hat. She saw flecks of sweat fly back from the team and she was forced to slow them. Just behind the hill where they turned off she saw a stream meandering along a valley. She had to let the team drink even though she didn't want to give Brindle and his men a chance to talk to them. Another drop of rain struck her as she stopped at the stream. She turned to Hadley. "Maybe you should get a drink."

"I can't move," he whispered hoarsely.

"Crawl in the back of the wagon and lie down so you don't fall out."

He nodded. Weakly he crawled over the seat and fell in a heap beside the tarp that covered his supplies.

"How will I know your place?"

"Red-roofed barn, a sod house, a windmill, and a small white frame house with red trim." He lifted his head. "Where's Brindle?"

She looked around with a frown. "I don't see him."

"Maybe he went on to Lincoln's place. It's north of here a ways. Or he could be hidin' up ahead just to give you a scare."

Maple shivered as she looked all around. Nothing moved on the vast prairie. The rain was closer though. She flicked the reins and urged the mares forward. She wanted to turn back toward town, but she didn't dare. Brindle could be just around a hill waiting for her to try.

Several minutes later thunder cracked and rain poured from the sky. Rain plastered her hair to her head and her wedding gown to her body. She glanced back to see Hadley's shirt pasted to his thin body. Was he unconscious? She couldn't tell. She turned back and urged the team forward. It was hard to see through the driving rain. The temperature dropped suddenly and the rain turned icy cold against her. She shivered. She longed for her rain gear, her boots, and the pants she wore when Momma didn't know.

In the back Hadley tried to lift his head but couldn't. He shivered with cold. His head spun and he couldn't tell if they were heading in the right direction.

She considered stopping and taking shelter under the wagon, but she knew Hadley needed a warm house and care.

At long last she caught sight of Hadley's place. She liked the look of it. It wasn't big like Papa's, but it was nice. She drove right up to the house and stopped.

Hadley weakly sat up. "We made it."

Maple jumped to the ground, swayed slightly, then found her legs and ran to the back of the wagon. She lifted out the end gate and helped Hadley out. "Lean on me."

Reluctantly he slipped his arm around her shoulders. Rain chilled him to the bone.

She circled his waist and walked him to the door. It opened into the kitchen. It was warm inside. She wrinkled her nose against the smell of their wet clothes as she eased him to a chair at the square oak table. "Where can I find dry clothes for you?"

"No need." He bit back a moan. "See to the team. I can tend myself."

"I doubt that! You look ready to pass out. Now, tell me where to find dry clothes for you."

"Bedroom."

She walked across the plank floor to the only other room of the house. A bed with a bright quilt on it took up most of the room. A humpback trunk stood at the end of the bed with a dresser against the wall beside a window. Clothes hung on pegs in the wall behind the door. She found clean longjohns that were almost worn out and took them for him to wear. There was no sense in his dressing more. He needed to get into bed before he caught a bad chill.

In the kitchen she held out the longjohns. "Can you manage?"

He didn't know if he could, but he wasn't about to let her help him. "I've been dressing myself since I was three years old."

She laughed and the sound surprised her. "I'll tend your wounds, then you get out of those wet things and get into bed."

"My team," he said weakly.

"I've been doing chores since I was three."

He grinned. "You'll find the salve in the washstand."

She moved the muslin curtain and looked on the shelf under the water bucket and washpan. She found the salve and a roll of bandages as well as a towel for him to dry himself. "After this I'll take care of your horses while you get into bed."

"I don't like this at all."

"I know how to take care of the horses."

"But you shouldn't have to." He tried to stand, then sank back down with a groan. "I'm sorry."

She swallowed hard. "I'm sorry they forced you to . . . to marry me."

"Think nothin' of it, miss. Buck Lincoln and his men will do anything to rile me up so I'll go after them."

She gently cleaned around the angry red wound on his arm. "How come?"

"I have a small spread he always claimed as his own. But I bought it and it's mine legal-like. He won't admit it."

"I haven't seen you before, have I?"

"Not that I know. I've heard of your pa. He won't let Buck Lincoln get away with this. Your pa will look for you."

She smiled and nodded. "Papa won't let anything bad happen to me if he can help it."

Hadley winced as she bandaged his arm. "What about the man you were set to marry?"

"Edward Turner, the banker."

"He seems old for you. And a real stuffed shirt."

"He is." She bit back a giggle, then carefully brushed his hair away from the wound on his head.

"Seems like you'd pick a rancher like your pa."

She studied him in surprise. "How do you know that?"

"You're not like town girls. You're a country girl full of courage and spunk."

"Why, thank you!" She smeared salve on his wound and covered it with the bandage. The smell of the salve turned her stomach. "Are you planning on marrying?"

"I have a mail-order bride I spoke for."

"Is she a country girl?"

He flushed. "No." But she was the only one who had answered his ad.

"I'm sorry, but I forgot your name."

"Hadley Clements. Some folks call me Hadd."

"I'm Maple Raines."

"I remember."

Maple pushed her tangled, wet hair back. "Momma would have a fit if she saw me . . . us now."

"She'd be thankful you were alive."

Maple bit her lip. "I don't know about that." She didn't want to think about Momma right now, so she quickly changed the subject. "Do your folks live around here?"

"About fifty miles away. I don't get to see much of 'em."

"It sounds like you miss them."

Hadley nodded. "I didn't want to move this far away from them, but I had a chance to buy my place at a good price, so I had to leave them."

"Do you have brothers and sisters?"

Hadley nodded, then swayed slightly.

She caught his arm. "You'd better change and lie down. I'll be back in as soon as I can."

He nodded. "Thank you, Maple."

She smiled and ducked back out into the rain. In the morning she would go back home where she belonged. Shivering, she climbed in the wagon and drove toward the barn.

CHAPTER 2

Rain lashing against her, Maple shivered and glanced behind her in the wagon. She frowned. She would have to unload the supplies before taking the wagon to the barn. With a shout to the team she turned them back toward the house. They obeyed instantly and she was impressed with how well Hadley had trained them. She jumped to the ground and cautiously opened the door. Thankfully Hadley wasn't changing his clothes in the kitchen. Quickly she unloaded the supplies, her hands blue with cold, then she drove to the barn, thankful for the shelter. The barn felt cold and smelled damp and musty. She unhitched the team and led them into separate stalls, fed them grain and carried buckets of water to them from the big wooden tank. A barn cat rubbed against her ankle and she smiled and bent down to pet it. At home the barn cats were too wild to touch. Momma had never allowed a cat in the house.

Maple stood in the doorway of the barn, reluctant to step out in the rain again. Taking a deep breath, she dashed across the yard, past a wooden bench near the clothes lines, then into the house. The house seemed chilly. She knew she had left the door open too long while carrying in the supplies. Shivering, she pulled off her ruined wedding shoes and frowned at the dirty wedding gown. She wanted to jerk it off. She listened for Hadley. Was he already in bed? Tiptoeing across the room, she peeked through the door and gasped in alarm. Hadley lay in a heap beside the bed. His matted hair covered one cheek and his dirty beard lay against his chest. The longjohns were pulled to his waist.

With a strangled cry she knelt beside him. He groaned and she jumped. "Can you hear me?"

His eyelids fluttered and slowly he opened his eyes. He looked at her without recognition.

"You must get into bed," Maple said firmly as she tried to help him up. She couldn't budge him. She left him and pulled back the top sheet, the blue blanket and the quilt. With a slight frown she turned back to him. He was watching her. "Get in bed."

Weakly he pushed himself up, holding onto his longjohns. She helped him into bed, then pulled the covers over him. He sighed heavily and closed his eyes.

She looked around for something dry to wear and found one of his shirts on a peg. She lifted it down and carried it to the kitchen. Quickly she undressed, dried off, and slipped on the shirt. It reached almost to her knees. She flushed as she darted a look toward the bedroom. It would be very embarrassing if he saw her now. But she knew he was too weak to leave his bed.

Her stomach growled with hunger and she realized she hadn't eaten since sometime yesterday. She had been too upset about the wedding to eat much the past few days. Quickly she started the fire, taking the chill off the room immediately, then looked for something to eat. She found canned peaches and ate a dish of them while she peeled potatoes. She cut up a few chunks of salt pork in a heavy cast iron skillet and started frying them, then added the sliced potatoes. The smell of frying pork and potatoes filled the house. Later she sat alone at the small table and ate. She couldn't remember a time in her life that she'd eaten alone. It felt good.

By late afternoon the rain stopped and a weak sun shone. Maple stepped outdoors and breathed in the fresh, rain-washed air. A warm wind blew against her bare legs and feet. Wouldn't Momma be aghast? A horse nickered in the barn. Cattle grazed in the pasture circled with the barbed wire Papa hated so much. The windmill squawked, then was silent. Beyond a sod house the blue sky stretched on and on, then touched the tops of the distant green hills. Slowly she walked away from the house toward small trees planted in rows. Were they fruit trees? She smiled. She'd always wanted fruit trees. She gently touched the leaves. "It's so peaceful here," she whispered, then giggled because she could shout at the top of her lungs and no one could hear her except Hadley. And he wouldn't because of his deep sleep. He'd said Brindle and his men had probably gone to Lincoln's ranch, so they were too far away to hear too.

Finally she walked back to the house. She left the door open for the fresh air. Hadley moaned and she hurried to the bedroom. He had flung off his covers, but was still asleep. She felt his forehead. "He's burning up!" she whispered hoarsely. She ran to get a bucket of cold water from the well, then carefully sponged his face and chest. His hair and beard were in the way.

He opened his eyes and muttered, "What're you doin' here?"

"Tryin' to get your fever down."

"I can take care of myself." His voice drifted off and he closed his eyes.

She washed his face again, redressed his wounds, and rubbed at his beard. It was dirty and tangled and she couldn't get it clean. Dare she cut it off?

With her head high she walked to the kitchen where she had seen scissors near the washpan. She would cut his beard and hair! Her heart racing, she snipped off a long strand of his beard and dropped it in the washpan. She cut his beard and mustache close to his face, then carefully cut his hair short enough to make it easy to wash. When she was finished she was surprised to see that he looked younger and was quite handsome.

He moaned and she fell back a step, her eyes wide and her heart racing. He didn't wake up. He flipped on his side, making it easy to cut the back of his hair. As quickly as she could she snipped it short. When he was awake and sitting on a chair she would even it up. She looked at the pile of hair in the washpan and suddenly realized how he might look at what she'd done. Her legs trembled. It was too late to undo what was done. He would have to live with it.

She spun around and strode from the bedroom, through the kitchen and outdoors. She ran out into the prairie and flung the water and the hair out. The wind caught it and carried it a short way before it fell to the ground. Her cheeks flushed, she ran to the house and closed the door after her. Taking a deep breath, she hurried to the bedroom to check on Hadley again. He was asleep, but still hot with fever. She carefully redressed his wounds. She heard him mutter in his sleep. It sounded like he was praying. It seemed strange to hear someone other than the pastor pray.

She glanced out the window to see the sun sinking in the west. What chores needed to be done? She'd have to see. She glanced down at her bare legs and feet. What could she find to wear outdoors? Spotting a pair of Hadley's denim pants, she pulled them on. They fit if she tightened the belt around her waist and cuffed up the legs. She slipped on her ruined wedding shoes and hurried to the barn. She turned the team out and watched them race across the pasture, then stop and roll over. She checked to make sure the tank was full of water, then locked the lever down to stop the windmill blades from turning. A guernsey cow bawled and headed for the barn. "He has a milk cow," she said in surprise. Many ranchers wouldn't bother with them. Papa had three because Momma had insisted. She said they needed their own butter, cream, milk, and cottage cheese. The ranch hands were glad of it too.

Maple found a bucket and milked the cow, then turned it back out to the pasture. In the house she strained the milk, poured it in a couple of big glazed clay jugs, corked them, and carried them to the well. She tied ropes around the handles and let them down into the cold water, then hurried back to the house. A coyote barked, then was quiet. It was almost dark outside and she closed and locked the door. She lit the lamp, sending a soft glow across the room.

Suddenly she felt too weary to stand and she drooped beside the table. The fire had gone out and the room was cool. Where would she sleep? Hadley slept in the only bed.

Sighing, she picked up the lamp and walked to the bedroom to find a blanket. She would sleep on the floor. After a few minutes of looking, she realized the only blankets were on the bed. She didn't dare take them from Hadley or he would get chilled. She stood beside the bed, the lamp held high. Hadley lay at the edge of the bed. Dare she crawl over him and sleep tight against the wall? Hooking her long, strawberry blonde hair over her ears, she stood there a long time trying to decide what to do. Hadley never moved from his spot. She must get some sleep in order to tend Hadley and do the chores tomorrow.

Trembling, she set the lamp on the dresser and blew it out. She pulled off the pants, but kept on the shirt. Enough moonlight shone through the window for her to find the bed and carefully crawl over Hadley's feet to the back. He moaned and she froze in place with her hand out to pull back the covers. He mumbled in his sleep but didn't move. She inched back the covers and slipped under them. Her head spun with fatigue. She closed her eyes with a long, low sigh. The heat from the covers and from Hadley soaked into her and she felt as if she was sinking deeper and deeper into the bed. It had been a long, terrible day—probably the worst day of her entire life.

Much later a suffocating heat woke her. She opened her eyes in the darkness and felt herself pressed tightly against Hadley. Her face flamed and she shot away from him and as close to the wall as she could get. She listened to his uneven breathing, then reached out cautiously and touched his face and forehead. He was burning with fever. She had to get his fever down immediately. She crept across his feet and quickly lit the lamp.

Maple held the lamp over him and saw the ashen look of his face and the pinched look around his mouth and nose. She had helped with hurt and sick cowboys before and she knew what to do. In the kitchen she filled the dipper with cold water and hurried back to Hadley. Lifting his head she dribbled water through his parched lips. His throat moved as he swallowed it. She sponged his face and chest with a cool cloth. Carefully she redressed his wounds and forced a few more drops of water down his throat. He seemed cooler and less fitful. She stood beside the bed for several minutes. Suddenly the room spun and she caught the headboard to keep from toppling over.

Once again she blew out the lamp and crawled over his feet. She eased under the covers and pressed tight against the wall. She closed her eyes and listened to him breathe. She would not move against him again! She was used to sleeping alone and taking up the whole bed, but she'd stay against the wall no matter what!

She woke gradually, feeling completely rested. Where was she? Her stomach cramped with hunger. She opened her eyes and her eyes locked with his. Her head was against his left shoulder and his arm curled around her, holding her to him.

He smiled. It felt good to wake up beside the woman who was his wife even though she was a stranger. He didn't want to frighten her, so he didn't speak.

She pushed against him and finally he released her. "Oh, dear! Oh! I'm so sorry!" She huddled against the wall, her face red. "I am so embarrassed!"

He grinned and his eyes crinkled at the corners. "Think nothin' of it." He was thinking more of it than he should have. He wanted a wife and kids. That's why he'd advertised for a mail-order bride two years ago.

Maple pushed her tangled hair from her flushed face. "You seem to be feeling better this morning."

"Seems like it." He felt light-headed, but that could be from Maple being so close.

She carefully crawled over his feet, turning hot than cold as she realized she still wore only his shirt. She quickly slipped on his pants and cinched the belt tight. "I'll get breakfast on." She started toward the kitchen, heard the bed creak, and slowly turned to make sure he was strong enough to stand on his own.

He sat on the side of the bed, trying to get the room to stop spinning. With a groan he rested his head in his hands, then cried out and rubbed frantically at his face. "My beard! What happened to it?"

She cleared her throat and fell back a step. "I . . . I cut it."

"What?" He pushed himself up, holding on to his longjohns. "You cut off my beard?"

"I couldn't get through it to cool off your face."

"A man's beard is his own!" He touched the close-cropped whiskers. "Why didn't you finish the job?"

She lifted her head and snapped, "I will next time!"

Fire leaped from his eyes. "I believe you would."

"It was dirty and nasty. I cut your hair as well."

He touched his head and shook his head. Suddenly he laughed. "You sure took advantage of me while I was helpless, didn't you?"

She bit her lip. Was he over his anger so quickly? "I reckon I did."

"I been too busy to take care of myself." He swayed and sank to the edge of the bed again. "Could be you'll have to drop me in the horse tank to give me a bath."

She laughed. "That's mighty cold water."

"It sure is."

She looked closely at him. "Are you all right?"

"I don't know as I am. My head's swimmin' some."

"You rest while I make breakfast. Get some food in you and you'll feel a whole lot better." She hurried to the kitchen and started the fire. She opened the door wide and let in fresh morning air. Chickens scratched in the yard. A meadowlark sang and a horse nickered. She saw the guernsey cow patiently waiting at the barn door. A few white clouds dotted the bright blue sky. She put coffee on to brew, then peeled a few potatoes to fry. Later she'd mix up a batch of bread. For now she stirred up pancake batter and quickly fried several pancakes. She turned to call Hadley to the table. He stood in the doorway watching her intently. Her heart turned over and she couldn't speak for a while. He wore faded blue pants and a checkered blue shirt with the sleeves rolled up. Finally she said, "Have a seat. Breakfast is ready."

He smiled, then walked slowly to the table and sat down. "I didn't know just how weak I was."

"You lost a lot of blood and you're fightin' a fever."

"I'll be all right once I eat. The food sure smells good."

"Thanks." She smiled as she poured their cups full of coffee and set the food in place. She sat down across from him and started to reach for her cup of coffee. He bowed his head and she quickly folded her hands in her lap, her cheeks pink.

"Heavenly Father, thank you for this food and for Maple for bein' so good as to fix it. Thank you for bringin' us here safely yesterday. Help me get Maple back to her folks." He hesitated. Did he want her to leave? Truth to tell, he liked having her here with him. He liked the way she could take charge and the courage she showed. He finished his prayer and lifted his head and smiled at her. "I welcome you to my home and my table."

"Thank you." She didn't know what to make of him.

"I'll take you back right after chores."

She frowned and shook her head. "You're too weak yet. I'm in no hurry."

"What about your . . . weddin'." He almost choked on the word.

She laughed. "I was glad to get out of it." As they ate she told him about Momma's desire for her to be married, especially to a man of prestige like Edward Turner.

Hadley swallowed the last of his pancakes. It had been a year since he'd eaten with someone and it felt good. "Couldn't you say no?"

She slowly set her coffee cup down. "I can't say no to Momma. She's . . . very strong-willed."

Hadley grinned and stroked his face. "Seems you are too."

Maple ducked her head. "I did overstep the bounds."

"No matter."

She looked at him in surprise. "I might as well trim your hair to get it even. And maybe shave off your beard. I always shaved Papa. I didn't do a very good job on you at all."

He trembled inside at the thought of her touching him so intimately. "Did you ever cut your Mr. Turner's hair or shave him?"

"Oh, my goodness, no!" She pressed her hand to her heart and shook her head. "And I hope I never do."

Hadley smiled. For some reason he hoped she never did either. "Your pa might come get you today."

"He doesn't know where I am."

"Somebody in Keene might know where my place is."

She didn't want to think about Papa coming to take her back to Ed Turner.

Hadley started to push back his chair. "I reckon I feel strong enough to do the chores."

Maple jumped up. "I reckon you don't! You march right back to bed!"

He laughed. "You sound like my ma."

"I'm sorry. I didn't mean to. But you don't dare exert yourself until your wounds are healed more."

He pushed himself up and the room spun. He gripped the back of his chair. "I feel as weak as a baby."

"See? Now, go to bed and I'll take care of chores."

"This hurts my pride, I hope you know."

She laughed. "It hurts my pride to have you see me like this."

He looked her up and down. Her hair was tangled

and she wore his clothes. "You look fine to me."

"I do?" she said weakly.

"As pretty as you did yesterday in your white gown."

She frowned and abruptly turned away. "You're teasing me." She grabbed up the milk pail and strode outdoors to milk the cow.

Slowly Hadley walked to the bedroom. He hadn't been teasing. She looked pretty with her hair down and the strained look of yesterday off her face. She wasn't the beauty that his sister, Diana, was or his half-sisters, Alane and Maureen were, but she was a good-looking woman, full of spunk.

Hadley sank to the edge of his bed. He felt as tired as if he'd worked a week without rest. "Heavenly Father, you are my strength and help. I need to get Maple back to her family. But I want her to have a happy life. Thank you for the wisdom to know what to do for her."

Outdoors Maple turned on the windmill and watched the blades spin in the hot wind. She milked the cow and turned it back to the pasture, found a few eggs in the nests in the barn, then carried the milk and eggs to the house. She should find out what else Hadley needed done. At home Papa's work was never done. His cowboys had fences to fix, horses to break, cattle to move from one pasture to another and haying to do.

In the kitchen Maple heard Hadley talking. She frowned. Was he out of his head? She listened closer. He was praying! She bit her lip. He was praying for her! She'd never heard anyone pray for her before. It felt strange. She strained the milk and washed the pail. What kind of man was Hadley Clements? He wasn't a preacher, yet he prayed to God as if he was used to doing such a strange thing. His voice faded away and she knew that he had fallen asleep.

She cleaned the kitchen, listening for sounds of anyone coming. Papa probably would come get her. But maybe one of Lincoln's hired hands had stayed on the look-out to keep anyone from coming. She shivered.

Later Maple braided her long hair to keep it out of her face, walked outdoors and pulled weeds that had grown up around the house. Slowly she walked to the sod house that stood to the west of the toilet. She peered inside the open door. Spider webs hung from the sagging rafters made of poles. A chicken scratched the dirt floor. Had Hadley lived in there before he'd built his frame house? Could she ever live in a sod house? She wrinkled her nose and shook her head.

A few minutes later she heated water and washed her clothes and a few things for Hadley. Maybe she could wear her wedding gown and undergarments instead of Hadley's clothes. She hung the limp white dress over the line and frowned. She didn't want to wear it again as long as she lived. But how could she stop Momma from forcing her to marry Edward Turner?

Her shoulders sagged as she sank to the bench. She might as well get used to the idea of being Mr.

Turner's wife. The wedding had been put off, but Momma wouldn't let anything—not even a marriage to Hadley Clements put it off again. A forced marriage couldn't be a real marriage in the sight of the law, could it?

Listlessly she walked to the fruit trees and touched them. Someday they'd be tall and full of apples and pears and peaches. But she wouldn't be around to see them. She frowned. Why was she acting as if it mattered? It didn't!

Later she folded the dry clothes and carried them inside. She considered putting on her dress, but couldn't stand the thought of it. She set the stack of folded clothes on the table just as Hadley walked in from the bedroom. He looked much better. She smiled. "Are you hungry?"

"I guess." He frowned as he looked out the window.

"What's wrong?"

He turned around, his hands on his hips, his eyes thoughtful. "I wonder why your pa didn't come for you? I hope nothing happened to him."

"I thought maybe Lincoln kept him away."

"That could be." Hadley's legs trembled. He walked slowly to a chair and sat at the table. He hated feeling so weak. "If there was law in the sandhills we wouldn't have to put up with Lincoln. He thinks he can still graze his cattle on range that belongs to me."

Maple sat across from Hadley and pushed the pile of clothes to the side of the table. "Does your mail-order bride know about the trouble you're having?"

"Yes."

"Where does she live?"

"St. Louis."

Maple wanted to get Hadley's mind off Buck Lincoln. "Tell me about her."

"From her letters she . . . Lucy Everett . . . sounds like a nice girl, easy to get to know."

Maple locked her fingers together in her lap. For some reason she was finding it hard to have Hadley say anything nice about Lucy Everett. "Do you . . . love her?"

Hadley flushed. "I need a wife. It gets mighty lonely for me."

"Shouldn't love enter into it?"

"You don't love that banker man."

"I know!" Maple's eyes flashed. "But Momma forced me into that. Who's forcing you?"

"Loneliness!" he said sharply. He sighed and shook his head. "Sorry. I been goin' back and forth about that very thing."

"Momma says there's more reasons to marry than just love."

"Do you always listen to Momma?"

Maple nodded.

Hadley saw the pain in Maple's eyes and decided to change the subject. "That's enough talk about things that make us feel bad." He rubbed his jaw, then fingered his uneven whiskers. "I've been givin' my face some thought."

Maple laughed. "Have you?"

"I reckon I'd like to be clean-shaven again the

way I was before I started bachin' here." He touched the bandage on his arm. "But I can't manage it myself. Reckon you could finish what you started?"

Maple jumped up. "I'll be glad to! I've been tryin' to picture you without that hair on your face." She flushed and turned quickly away to pour hot water into the washpan.

Hadley saw her flush and grinned. "Don't be embarrassed on my account. I been wonderin' the same thing. My family would laugh at me if they saw me with long hair and a scruffy beard."

"Tell me about your family."

He looked off across the table, seeing another house—a house full of his family. "My real ma died when my brother, Worth, was three. Diana was four and I was six. Morgan Clements, my pa, married the schoolteacher, Laurel Bennett, and he brought her home as our ma. We didn't know he was plannin' on bringin' us a new ma. It was hard gettin' used to her, but we learned to love her and so did Pa." Hadley smiled as he remembered the fun they'd all had together. "Ma and Pa have four kids of their own—Garrett, Forster, Alane, and Maureen. They built two more bedrooms and a big dining room onto their house. It was always full of love and laughter and music."

"Mine was mostly quiet," Maple whispered.

"Diana's married, but lives on a ranch nearby. The others are still at home."

"I always wanted brothers and sisters." Maple sighed as she carried the straight razor and the pan of hot water to the table. Wood snapped in the cast iron stove. Dust particles danced in the late afternoon sunshine streaming through the window. "When I get married I want lots of kids so they never get lonely like I did."

Hadley almost reminded her she was married—to him, but instead he watched her lather the soap and rub it on his face. His pulse quickened at her touch. Could she tell?

She drew the razor down his jaw, then sloshed the blade in the hot water. The skin under his beard was lighter tanned than his face. She shaved him just as she'd shaved her papa. She soaked a cloth in hot water, wrung it out, and laid it over his face for a minute. She lifted it off and patted him dry. She liked the look of his square chin.

He squirmed at her close inspection. "Should I put a bag over my head?"

She laughed. "No. I can't imagine why you let your beard and hair grow."

He shrugged. "It was bothersome to shave every day. And it kept my face warm in the winter."

"I wonder if your mail-order bride would like you with a beard."

Hadley shrugged. "I been thinkin' I probably made a mistake sending for her."

"Why do you say that?"

He shook his head. He couldn't very well tell Maple now that he'd seen her in his kitchen and in his bed he couldn't picture anyone else there. She wouldn't want to hear that's how he felt. He hadn't realized it until now. He stood up slowly to keep from getting dizzy. He didn't dare let her stay any longer or he'd never be able to let her go. He looked at her with a stubborn look on his face. "First thing in the mornin' we're headin' for Keene."

"But you're not strong enough!"

"Your family will be worried about you."

"I know. I don't want to marry Ed Turner," she whispered with her head down and her shoulders slumped.

"Then don't!"

She carried the washpan outdoors and flung the water and hair out in a wide arc. She strode back inside and looked squarely at Hadley. "There's no use discussing it. I will marry him." She set the pan in place beside the water bucket. "Momma'll be madder than a wet hen that I've been gone this long. She'll blame it on me."

"I'll tell her it was my fault. I'll make her understand."

"You can't, but thanks for offering."

His jaw tightened. He'd talk to Momma all right! He forced himself to relax. He wanted to put a smile back on Maple's face. "Do you play checkers?"

She grinned. "Am I Ben Raines' daughter? Of course I play! Why do you ask?"

"I figured since I can't do anything but sit quietly we could have a game or two of checkers. That's another thing I miss."

"Sure, I'd like a game." It would take her mind off going back home.

Hadley pulled a checker board and checkers from the bottom of the cupboard and set them on the table. He spilled the checkers from the box onto the wooden board. "Red or black?"

"Red." She reached for the checkers just as he pushed them toward her. Their hands brushed and her pulse tingled. She quickly put her checkers in place, her cheeks bright spots of red.

He put his checkers in place without a word.

Wood popped in the stove and she jumped, then laughed. "I don't know what's wrong with me. I'm usually not so jumpy."

He managed to smile at her without showing her how she made his heart beat faster. "You've been through a lot. We'll relax, play a few games, then make plans for tomorrow."

She nodded. Did she really want to go home? Of course she did! She couldn't continue to stay with this stranger.

CHAPTER 3

Maple folded her hands in her lap and watched a fly land on the bay mare's ear. The mare flicked her ear and knocked the fly off. A prairie chicken flew up from the ground and skimmed the top of the waving prairie grass. The blue sky stretched on for miles, then dipped down to touch the rolling hills. The sun was about an hour from being directly overhead. She glanced at Hadley from under the wide-brimmed brown hat he'd given her to wear. His hat, almost like hers, shielded his expression from her. He had been quiet most of the two hours they were traveling. Was he glad to be rid of her? A loneliness she couldn't understand filled her. She bit her lip to keep it from trembling. She wasn't one to cry. Why did she feel like she'd burst into tears at the drop of a hatpin? Keene was just ahead. A few miles past the town was Papa's ranch. She'd be back home where she could change from Hadley's pants to her own clothes. She would be home again, sleep in her own bed, eat food Carla prepared.

Up ahead Maple spotted the church and her stomach tightened. Pictures of the horror that had taken place just days before flashed across her mind.

Hadley had lifted her veil and kissed her. Her lips burned and she couldn't look at Hadley in case he could read her thoughts. The man who had kissed her seemed different from the man sitting beside her. What would she do if he kissed her now? She scowled and pressed her lips tightly together.

A dust devil whirled from the sod schoolhouse across to the church. Maple saw herself in her wedding gown beside Ed Turner at the altar. Would she stand at the altar in a few days with Mr. Turner to exchange marriage vows? She shivered and wrapped her arms about herself.

Hadley drove past the church down the deserted street. He couldn't look at the church or he might shout for her to defy Momma and refuse to marry Edward Turner. Hadley gripped the reins and watched the dust billow up. He had no right to interfere in Maple's life. She was his wife only on paper. Soon that would be erased just like the marks on a slate.

Maple saw Papa's buggy outside the general store. She sucked in her breath. Had he been on his way to find her? "There's Papa's buggy," she said in a strained voice.

Hadley touched her hand and forced a smile. "Don't be scared. He'll be glad you're back."

She managed to smile as Hadley stopped the wagon near the store. Pulling off her hat she slapped dust from her shirt and denim pants. One long strawberry blonde braid hung down her thin back.

Hadley dropped to the ground, then held his arms out to her. Could he really let her go?

Hesitantly she reached for him and rested her hands on his strong shoulders. She felt him stiffen.

Hadley circled her waist with his hands and stood her on the ground. He looked deep into her eyes, then stepped back and motioned for her to walk ahead of him onto the plank sidewalk. He hadn't felt this sad even when he'd left home for his own place or when the dog he had from the time he was seven was killed by a wildcat. This was a whole new depth of feeling he didn't know was inside him. In silent anguish he cried out for God to give him the strength to do what was right.

Her legs trembling, Maple walked ahead of Hadley. She felt the warmth of his body behind her and heard the thud of his boots on the walk.

Just then Ben and Leona Raines stepped from the general store. Maple stopped short. She knew they hadn't noticed her. Ben wore his worn levis and a blue plaid shirt. Leona wore a dark green dress and hat.

"You can face them," Hadley whispered close to her ear. "I'll be right beside you."

Maple wanted to take his hand, but she didn't.

Ben turned his head and saw Maple. The color drained from his face and he couldn't speak. He nudged Leona.

"Maple!" Leona whispered, swaying slightly.

Ben circled her waist for support as they hurried toward Maple.

"Maple!" they cried, both trying to hug her at the same time.

Ben rubbed a tear from his eye. "Are you all

right?"

"Yes," Maple whispered.

Leona looked sharply at Hadley. "Who is this man? Who are you?"

"Hadley Clements." He bit back a chuckle, knowing he looked very different than the scarecrow Maple had married.

"You can't be!" Leona shook her head and turned back to Maple. "Who is he?" She sounded very suspicious.

"This is the man I married," Maple said with a laugh. "He did have long hair and a beard."

Hadley grinned and suddenly felt mischievous. "Maple shaved off my beard, cut my hair, and made me clean up."

Leona gasped.

Ben looked from Maple to Hadley and back again, then grinned.

"I would have brought Maple back sooner, but I'd been shot and was under the weather a while. Maple nursed me back to health and here we are!" Hadley smiled down at Maple. "I could have died without her care."

Maple smiled and shook her head.

Leona cleared her throat. "Mr. Turner will be glad to see you're back. He wanted to ride after you, but Brindle's man wouldn't let him."

"Did they hurt him?" Maple asked.

Ben shook his head. "None of us were hurt, but we couldn't leave town for a while. When Ed returned he had to go about his business as usual."

Hadley clenched his fists. Nothing would have

kept him from riding after *his* bride!

"He'll want to set another wedding date as soon as possible," Leona said crisply. "I asked the pastor about the marriage between . . . the two of you."

Maple's heart stopped, then raced on.

A muscle in Hadley's jaw jumped.

"He said you just have to sign an annulment paper," Leona said. "Then you'll be free to marry Mr. Turner."

Maple trembled. Wasn't this what she'd expected all along? Why was it suddenly so alarming?

"But we won't worry about that now," Ben said. "We're just glad to see you're both well."

Leona looked Maple up and down and clicked her tongue. "You're a sight!"

"She looks fine to me," Hadley said.

Leona scowled at him before she turned back to Maple. "I won't allow Mr. Turner to see you in such a state. Get in the buggy and we'll get you home."

"She'll ride with me!" Hadley wasn't going to ride away without another word like Leona Raines expected him to do. Maple needed his help and he planned to give it to her.

Maple looked at Hadley in surprise. She thought he would be glad to be rid of her so he could get back to a normal life.

"Stay for dinner with us, Hadley." Ben took Leona's arm as he smiled at Hadley. "I want a chance to thank you proper for saving Maple."

Leona frowned, but before she could speak Edward Turner stepped out of the bank. He wore a dark suit and stiff white collar.

Maple shrank back and bumped into Hadley. She stayed there, finding strength in the warmth and hardness of his body.

Hadley caught Maple's hand and held it. He felt her tremble and vowed that he would do anything to keep her from being forced to marry Ed Turner.

"Maple!" Ed cried as he hurried toward her, his short legs pumping up and down. He saw the tall stranger holding Maple's hand and anger shot through him. "Just who are you, mister?"

"Maple's husband. Hadley Clements." It took all of Hadley's will power to keep from knocking Ed down.

Ed's face turned brick-red. "You won't be her husband much longer."

Leona caught Ed's arm and smiled. "I'll bring Maple back tomorrow after she's had a chance to rest and clean up. We'll set the new wedding date then."

"We're headin' home now. This is not the time to talk about it." Ben tried to urge Leona on.

Maple bit her lip. If only she could speak up to tell Mr. Turner she would never be his wife! She looked helplessly at Hadley. He winked at her and she felt a little better.

"We'll be talkin' to you in a few days, Turner." Ben managed to tug Leona away from Ed.

Ed mumbled goodbye and walked stiffly back toward the bank.

Leona frowned at Ben. "You weren't much help." She shook her finger at Maple. "Young lady,

I don't know what happened to your manners, but you'd better remember them the next time we see Mr. Turner."

"Yes, Momma," Maple whispered.

Hadley turned her toward the wagon. "We'll see you at the ranch." He helped Maple up into the wagon and climbed up beside her. He flicked the reins against the bays. They stepped forward and the wagon jerked, then rolled along the dusty street.

"Are you mad?" Maple asked.

"Yes! At your momma for making you seem like a little kid."

Maple looked at Hadley in surprise. He was taking her side against Momma! Maple tried to think of something to say, but couldn't. A dog barked at the left back wheel. Wind blew a tumbleweed across the road and into the cemetery.

"I hope you won't ever forget me," Hadley said as he drove out of town and followed the wagon trail Maple said was the way to the ranch.

She smiled. "I reckon I won't."

He grinned and rubbed his jaw. "I won't forget the shave and the haircut."

"That was pretty bold of me."

"I'm glad you did it."

She laughed. "Me too."

Just then they passed a lone cottonwood with wide spreading branches. "We're on the Double R now," Maple said.

"Your papa has every right to be proud of his place."

"He worked hard building it up to what it is today." Maple sighed heavily. "He always wanted a son to leave it to."

"Maybe you'll give him a grandson."

Maple flushed. She didn't want to think about having children with Ed Turner.

He saw he'd embarrassed her and he wanted to put her at ease again. "Show me the tree you climb to count stars." She had told him about it last night when they were sitting on the bench and looking at the stars. He had always had family to talk to and sit outside with, but she'd spent most of her free time by herself.

Maple smiled self-consciously. "The trees all look alike."

"I don't care. I want to carry home with me a picture of you sittin' in your special tree."

"Since you asked, I'll show you." Not even Papa had ever asked about her special tree.

Hadley smiled at her. "I wish we could sit on the branch together tonight and count stars. I could take that home with me."

Why was he talking like that to her? She was a stranger to him. "I figured you'd want to get right back to your place. What about your night chores?"

"I'll get back in time for them. I can do them after dark if I have to."

She frowned and clicked her tongue. "I didn't get the ironing done for you."

"No need. I'll wear my shirts wrinkled." He grinned. "Who'll see me?"

Maple sighed heavily. "I don't know what I'll

say to Momma about the time I spent with you."

"You did the chores and took care of me. That's enough to tell."

"You don't know Momma." Maple shivered even though the morning sun was hot.

"I'll be prayin' for you."

"Thanks." She didn't know what else to say.

Just around the hill Hadley drove into a wide valley. He saw the large two-story white frame house with a brass bell hanging from a wooden beam in the front yard. There were three barns, several sheds, and a corral with a herd of horses milling around. Hadley whistled in admiration. "This is quite a place! I've heard about your pa's horses. I'll like seein' them up close."

"He'll like showin' them to you." Maple looked over her shoulder at the buggy behind them just far enough away to miss their dust. She turned around as Hadley drove toward the hitching rail near the white picket fence circling the house and the well-trimmed grassy yard. Several large cottonwoods shaded the area. "There's Momma's flower garden." Bright flowers were in bloom. Maple pointed to the south of the house. "And just in back of that, her vegetable garden. She's proud of her gardens. We'll probably have fresh green beans for dinner."

Hadley stopped at the hitching rail. "And where's your special tree?"

Maple smiled as she pointed to the tree at the corner of the house. The cottonwood stood about a hundred feet tall and had a trunk about four feet through with wide branches going out from it. The leaves twirled and danced, making a gentle sound. "See the second branch? It was made to sit on."

Hadley nodded. "We'd both fit on it. Let's climb up right now and pretend the stars are out."

Maple shook her head, then giggled and whispered, "The stars would be circling our heads if Momma caught us doin' that."

Ben stopped the buggy beside the wagon. Before he could move, Leona climbed out and strode to Maple's side of the wagon.

"Come inside and get out of those ridiculous clothes!"

Maple looked helplessly at Hadley. "Please don't leave without sayin' goodbye."

"I won't." He wanted to shield her against Momma, but right now he didn't know how he could.

"He's stayin' for dinner," Ben said. "Aren't you, Hadley?"

"Sure am." Hadley grinned and nodded.

"Come on, Maple!" Leona stood with her hands at her wide waist and a frown on her face. "Carla will have dinner on soon."

Maple jumped to the ground, sending puffs of dust on her worn-out wedding shoes. She watched Papa take Hadley toward the corral, then reluctantly walked inside with Momma. The wide hallway looked just the same. The grandfather clock sounded loud. Maple smelled fried chicken and fresh-baked bread.

Leona rushed Maple up the wide stairs to the

room she'd had since she was a little girl. The wallpaper was pale yellow with pink roses in tidy rows between thin pink stripes. A large four-poster bed stood out from the wall with a heavy chest at the foot. A full length beveled looking glass with a wide oak frame hung on the wall beside a large wardrobe. A pink and yellow sofa faced a brick fireplace that was used only in the dead of winter. The room was almost as big as Hadley's whole house.

Maple saw the bag she'd packed to take on her honeymoon and she shuddered.

"I thought about unpacking it," Leona said, brushing at a tear with one hand and touching the bag with the other. "I was so afraid something dreadful had happened to you. Your papa rode after you, but when he came back without you, I thought I might never see you again!"

"I'm just fine, Momma."

"I know. I thought Brindle might kill you. I was so frightened for you!"

Maple looked at Momma in surprise. Momma really cared!

Leona took a deep breath. "You're home now. I want to hear all about your time with that . . . horrible man."

"He saved my life, Momma."

Just then Carla, the housekeeper, knocked and carried in hot water for Maple. Carla was short and slight but almost as strong as the cowboys. Her dark hair hung in two braids over her shoulders and she looked as if she had Indian blood. "I am glad you're home safe and sound, Maple."

"Thank you, Carla." Maple . smiled. She and Carla got along fine.

Carla poured the water into a basin and set the heavy pitcher on the commode. "Dinner will be ready in fifteen minutes."

"We'll be right there." Leona laid out a lacy pantalet for Maple. "Hurry now."

"I will, Momma."

Leona studied Maple, then finally turned and walked out.

Maple peeled off Hadley's pants and shirt, washed, then dressed in the lacy pantalets, soft white chemise, and a green delaine dress covered with tiny flowers. She buttoned the small green buttons up the bodice, slipped on black shoes with a low heel, then twisted and turned in front of the looking glass. She'd pass. She brushed her hair, piling it up and pinning it in place with combs and pins. She looked very different than she had minutes before. What would Hadley think of her now? She wrinkled her nose. He probably wouldn't notice.

Taking a deep breath, she lifted her skirts slightly and walked downstairs. She heard Hadley talking in the parlor. Her stomach fluttered. She stopped next to the red velvet chair that stood beside a mahogany table in the hallway. Hadley's hat hung on the halltree next to Papa's. Maple bit her lip and stepped into the parlor. Her parents sat on the dark blue velvet sofa Momma had ordered from New York City two years ago. Looking at ease,

Hadley sat across from them in a blue chair. He smiled and jumped up when he saw Maple. She smiled and stepped to his side.

"You look beautiful," Hadley said softly. Indeed she looked lovely, but he favored her in his clothes with her hair down.

Maple blushed. She couldn't look at Momma to see what expression was on her face.

Ben kissed Maple's cheek. "You do look very nice."

Leona lifted her chin. "Dinner is on already. Let's eat it before it's cold." She walked into the hall and to the dining room.

Maple followed, conscious of Hadley right behind her with Papa. The dining room was large. The table, covered with a white linen cloth, seemed to stretch on forever with high-backed oak chairs slipped up under it. Carla had set only one end of the table to make the meal cozier. Steaming fried chicken, mashed potatoes, green beans, slices of fresh-baked bread, a fruit salad, and a platter of raw vegetables filled the end of the table. Tall goblets of water stood near each delicate blue flowered china plate. A white linen napkin was folded neatly under each fork. The delicious aromas filled the room.

Hadley held Maple's chair, then sat beside her and across from Leona. Ben sat at the head of the table. Hadley suddenly missed his family. Their dining room table was large also, but it was always filled with family and friends. And there was seldom the tension in the air that he felt here.

Leona cleared her throat. "Mr. Clements, will you say grace?"

Maple frowned. What was Momma up to? They never prayed before they ate. Was she trying to put Hadley on the spot?

Hadley bowed his head. "Heavenly Father, thank you for your great blessings to us. Thank you for Jesus. Bless this home in a special way. Bless Maple and help her to know her own heart. Thank you for this food set before us. May it be nourishment to our bodies. In Jesus' Name. Amen."

Hiding a smile, Maple peeked at the surprised look on Momma's face. Just then Hadley bumped Maple's leg with his and winked. He knew what Momma had tried to do! Maple bit back a giggle. She saw the twinkle in Hadley's eye and she knew he was holding back a chuckle.

Ben held the platter of chicken out to Leona and said to Maple, "Hadd told me how you nursed him back to health. I'm proud of you, daughter."

"What's this?" Leona asked sharply.

"He'd been shot, Momma. He had a fever. We told you."

"You taught her how to nurse sick folks, Mrs. Raines." Ben forked a piece of breast meat onto Leona's plate and passed it to Hadley. "You should be proud of your daughter."

Leona shot a piercing look at Hadley, then at Maple. "Is there something I don't know?"

Maple stiffened. "No, Momma."

"You'd better not try to keep anything from me!"

Anger rose in Hadley. Carefully he set the platter of chicken down beside the bowl of mashed potatoes. He hated to see Maple frightened of her own mother. He wanted to take her away where she could be herself. He wanted her with him! "I'm sure Maple hasn't told you we shared a bed for three nights."

Maple stared in horror at Hadley. What had come over him to say such a thing?

Leona sputtered and dropped her fork with a clatter. Ben coughed, his face red. The clock chimed one, then all was silent.

"I'm sorry, Maple," Hadley said softly. "I shouldn't have said that."

"Then why did you?" Maple struggled to hold back tears.

"I can see by Maple's face it's true," Leona snapped. She shook her finger at Maple. "Why didn't you tell me you are husband and wife completely? How dare you lead me to believe you'll marry Mr. Turner?"

Maple ducked her head and moaned.

Hadley narrowed his eyes. "Mrs. Raines, you're talkin' to my wife in a manner I won't allow! She doesn't have to tell you anything unless she wants to." Leona started to speak, but Hadley continued. "We planned to tell you she wouldn't marry Mr. Turner no matter what you wanted."

Leona turned to Ben. "Say something! Don't just sit there!"

"What is there to say? What's done is done." Smiling, Ben slowly stood and held his hand out to

Hadley. "Welcome to the family. I couldn't have picked a better man for my daughter."

"What?" Leona cried, her face red, then white.

Hadley smiled with pleasure as he shook hands. He liked Ben.

Maple stared at Papa and at Hadley, then shot out of her chair. This was just too much! "Hadley Clements, I will not stay married to you!"

"Watch your tongue, girl," Ben snapped.

Maple ignored Ben as she glared at Hadley. "I'm not goin' back with you now or ever!"

Hadley stared at her in surprise. He thought she'd go along with his plan to keep from marrying Ed Turner.

Leona leaned forward, her eyes flashing. "You will indeed go home with him! You brought this on yourself. No other man will ever have you now. You're married to this man and you'll stay married to him!"

"She's right," Ben said firmly. "No daughter of mine will leave her husband. Not when he's a good man like Hadd here."

Shaking her head helplessly, Maple ran from the room.

Hadley strode after her and caught her arm just as she started up the stairs.

"Listen to me, Maple."

She tried to jerk free, but his grip was too tight. "No! How could you do this to me? I was beginning to trust you!"

"Going with me is better than stayin' here. Or marryin' Ed Turner."

"How can you say that?"

"You liked being at my place. Didn't you?"

"You're forcing me to go with you just like Momma's forced me to do things all my life. Nothing's changed!"

Hadley sighed heavily and dropped his hand to his side. "I'm sorry. I didn't mean for it to work like this."

She gingerly rubbed her arm where she could still feel his touch.

"Think about it, Maple." He reached out to her, but she jerked away. He rested his hand on the shiny bannister. "At first I thought I could let you go, but when I saw how your mother and Ed Turner treated you, I knew I couldn't."

She lifted her chin. "You don't have to feel sorry for me!"

"Don't twist my words!" He caught her hand and wouldn't let her pull away. "I'll be a good husband to you. With God's help we'll grow to love each other."

His words and his touch sent shivers over her. "You can't force me to love you," she whispered hoarsely.

"I don't intend to." He smiled gently. "I promise I'll be a good husband."

She flushed painfully and shook her head.

"Don't fret about it now. Let's go eat dinner."

"No! I can't face them!"

"Sure you can."

"I can't."

"I'm with you."

She sighed.

"After dinner you pack your things and we'll leave."

She trembled. Why fight it? She had to go with him with Momma and Papa both on Hadley's side. Slowly she walked back to the table and sat down.

"Now, let's eat," Leona said as she handed the dish of mashed potatoes to Hadley. "Maple, I'm not one to cry over spilt milk as you know. I've decided to send a couple of rose bushes for you to plant at your place. I thought you'd like that."

Maple nodded as she spooned a few green beans on to her plate. Could she eat now or ever?

"Your trunk is already packed, so that won't be a problem." Momma talked on and on about what Maple could take.

Maple thought of the town clothes in the trunk. The clothes weren't made to do chores in. She didn't say anything in case Momma insisted they stop in town and buy suitable work clothes. She didn't want to see Mr. Turner again or explain to others in town why she was willingly going with Hadley.

Later when the wagon was loaded, Ben took Maple in his arms and whispered in her ear, "You'll have a good life with this man."

Maple bit back a sharp answer. She thought Papa would be on her side.

"He suits you. I checked him out and he's a fine man. Don't be afraid to love him and let him love you."

"Oh, Papa." She'd never agree to that! She pulled away from Papa and hugged Momma. It was harder to leave than she thought. "Come visit us, Momma."

Leona hugged Maple fiercely. "We will. As soon as we can!"

"You can bet on it," Ben said with a nod. He turned to Hadley and shook his hand. "I hope Buck Lincoln has the sense to leave you alone."

"He'll have to give up sooner or later. I'm not movin' no matter what."

Leona shook her finger at Hadley. "Don't you put my daughter in danger!"

"I'll take good care of her."

"He sure will," Ben said, smiling.

Maple glanced at Hadley, then quickly away. He was her husband! She would share his ranch with him and even fight Buck Lincoln with him. A bubble of excitement popped inside her, surprising her, but she quickly squelched it. She was not going to enjoy living with Hadley Clements!

Slowly she climbed up on the wagon seat, locked her hands over her drawstring purse, and looked around at the ranch she had lived on all her life. When would she see her home again? She looked at the cottonwood where she had often sat to count stars or daydream. A lump lodged in her throat.

Leona stepped close to the wagon. "Make sure you keep that burlap wet around the roots of the rose bushes."

"I will, Momma."

Hadley smiled at Ben and Leona, then leaped up beside Maple. "God bless you both. Don't worry about your daughter. I intend to take good care of her."

Maple pressed her lips tightly together and looked straight ahead.

CHAPTER 4

In Keene Hadley stopped at the general store, looped the reins around the brake handle, and turned to Maple. Wind pressed his shirt against his chest and almost blew off his hat. "Is there anything you want while we're in town?"

Her back stiff and her eyes straight ahead, Maple shook her head. The wind tugged at her yellow and brown bonnet, but it was tied securely under her chin and couldn't blow off. She wanted to get out of town as quickly as possible before anyone stopped to talk to her. She didn't see anyone on the street except two boys playing marbles in a sandy circle.

"Do you want to come in?"

"No."

Hadley dropped to the ground and smiled up at her. "I'll be right back." His boots thudded on the plank sidewalk as he walked to the door and on inside the store.

Just then Mrs. Grove and Mrs. Boston started past the wagon, then stopped. Wind billowed out their calico dresses. They said hello to Maple. She nodded her head. After a minute they walked on, whispering to each other. Maple flushed. She wanted to pull her bonnet low over her face. A horse neighed. Two bare-footed girls ran down the street rolling a hoop. Ed Turner walked from the bank and turned toward the wagon. His face was brick-red and his black suit coat flapped at his thick middle. Maple froze. She wanted to duck under the seat, but she sat still and waited.

"What's all this, Maple?" Ed asked stiffly as he motioned to the things loaded in the back of the wagon.

"My things." Her voice came out in a weak croak.

"And where are you taking them?"

She wanted to yell at him to mind his own business, but she said in an even voice, "To my home. Hadley Clements' home."

Ed bit his lip and ran his finger under his stiff collar. "What about . . . me?"

"You're too late," Hadley said behind him.

The color drained from Ed's round face as he slowly turned to face Hadley. "Too late?"

"To marry her. She's my wife now and forever." Hadley pushed a brown parcel under the wagon seat, then leaped up beside Maple. "Good day, Mr. Turner." Hadley slapped the reins against the bays.

"If you need me, I'll be here for you, Maple," Ed called as the wagon rolled away.

Maple didn't acknowledge that she'd heard him. She was glad her bonnet hid her face.

Hadley drove without speaking. Silently he prayed for Maple. He knew going with him was hard on her. After a long time Hadley said, "You look beautiful, Maple."

She moved agitatedly. "Don't say that!"

"It's true!"

She knotted her fists and glared at him. "I am not a beautiful woman."

"Yes, you are. One of these days I'll make you believe it."

She shook her head and turned her face from him. She watched a pack of coyotes slink out of sight behind a low hill. A hawk screeched as it soared across the bright blue sky.

At Grassy River Hadley stopped to water the bays. "Want to stretch your legs?"

Maple stubbornly shook her head.

He shrugged and dropped to the ground. He soaked down the burlap on the rose bushes. A kill-deer cried out and ran its funny long-legged run across the sand. Maple glanced at Hadley as he bent down to dip his neckerchief in the water. It would feel good to sponge off her hot, dusty face. He wrung out his neckerchief, dabbed his face, then wiped the sweat band of his hat. He dropped his hat in place and took a step toward the wagon.

Suddenly a rattlesnake whirred in warning. Hadley froze.

Maple saw the coiled snake and her heart stood still. The whole world stood still. She pulled the rifle from the boot beside the wagon seat, aimed, and fired. Her ears rang with the noise. The bullet struck the snake, sending it flying.

Hadley jumped away from the dead snake and caught the neck strap of the nearest bay as it started to rear in fright. Hadley blew out his breath, then smiled at Maple. "Thanks."

She nodded as she slowly slipped the rifle in the boot. Inside she was trembling, but she'd learned long ago how to hide her inner turmoil.

He climbed up beside her and took her hands in his. "Thank you!"

She pulled her hands free. "It was nothing."

"I owe you my life again. Ask me for anything and I'll give it to you."

She bit her lip and looked him right in the eyes. "Let me go back home."

His heart plunged to his feet. "No. I can't."

"You said ask anything!"

"But not that. I can't live without you, Maple. You're my wife! I would never let you go back to that banker or to your momma!"

She turned her head away from him and stared at the endless prairie and the wide blue sky dotted with puffs of cottony clouds.

Hadley sat still for a long time, then finally urged the team forward. Had he made a mistake forcing her to come with him? Would she hate him all her life? Silently he prayed for her and for them.

Maple sat in silence the rest of the way to Hadley's place. Darkness fell just as he stopped the team near the house. She climbed out before he could help her.

Inside the house Hadley struck a match and lit the lamp. Smell of sulfur and kerosene were strong for a minute, then the warm breeze blowing through the open door blew it away. A cricket chirped in a far corner. The bays moved restlessly, rattling their harness. Hadley turned to Maple. "Welcome home. Rest while I unload the wagon."

She lifted her chin. "I'm capable of helping."

His heart sank. This wasn't going to be the honeymoon he'd planned on. Outside he lifted down the maple rocking chair and carried it to a corner of the kitchen. He'd always wanted a rocker in that corner. At home Ma and Pa had rockers near the fireplace and they sat together each evening, talking over the day and reading the Bible to the family. He wanted the same for him and Maple.

She lifted out the rose bushes and set them by the well. Pumping a bucket of water, she poured it over the burlap at the base of the bushes. Tomorrow she'd plant them on the south side of the house.

In silence Hadley lifted down the looking glass while she grabbed a portmanteau and carried it to the bedroom. She almost bumped into Hadley and quickly stepped aside. Together they hoisted out the oblong tub with four sturdy legs. Momma had insisted they take it at the last minute.

"We'll set it against the house until I find a place for it," Hadley said.

The tub was heavier than it looked and Maple's muscles strained. In relief she lowered it to the ground. Tomorrow while Hadley was away from the ranch she'd fill it with warm water and soak in it until all the aches from traveling were gone.

When everything was unloaded Hadley picked up the milk pail and set it in the wagon. "I'll milk before I come in."

"I'll make supper."

"I'm not hungry."

She shrugged. "I'm not either." She was too nervous about tonight to eat.

"Don't bother fixin' anything then." Hadley walked to the head of the bays and led them to the barn.

Slowly Maple walked inside, closing the screen door against moths. In the bedroom she unpacked the few things she'd need for the night. She looked at the bed and her stomach cramped painfully. Abruptly she turned away and grabbed up a brush. Slowly she brushed her hair and braided it for the night. She undressed and slipped on her soft nightdress. She quickly pulled her robe on and tied the belt around her thin waist. She heard Hadley come in and strain the milk. She whimpered, suddenly feeling like a caged animal.

Hadley stood in the kitchen and looked at the closed bedroom door. He wanted to push open the door and take his rightful place in his bed as Maple's husband, but the fearful look in her eyes flashed across his mind. He couldn't force her to love him. He sighed heavily and looked at the heap of bedding on the rocking chair that they had unloaded from the wagon. He could make himself a bed on the kitchen floor. Slowly he walked to the bedroom door and knocked.

Maple froze, her hand at her racing heart. "Yes?"

Hadley opened the door. His pulse leaped at the sight of her. But he saw the fear in her eyes and he knew he was doing the right thing. "I need to get some things. I'll sleep on a pallet in the kitchen."

She bit back a gasp. Relief washed over her, then she frowned as she watched him get clean clothes. Why had he decided not to share the bed with her? Didn't he want her after all? Had he seen how ugly she was and how unlovable?

He smiled at her. "Good night, Maple."

"Good night," she whispered.

He walked to the door, hesitated, and stepped back to her side. He took her hand.

She stiffened and her heart thundered.

"I'd like us to pray together."

Before she could answer, he bowed his head. She stared at him in shock. Pray together! What a strange thing to do. Finally she bowed her head.

"Father in heaven, thank you for bringing us home safely. I'm glad you love us and watch over us always. Bless Maple. Give her a good night's rest. Help us to grow more like you each day. And teach us to love one another. In Jesus' Name. Amen."

The prayer touched Maple as nothing had ever done. When she was a little girl she had accepted Jesus as her Savior, but never learned the next step to take. Hadley must have. God was real to him. She lifted her eyes. He would be able to tell her how to reach God.

Hadley lowered his head and touched his lips to hers in a soft, tender kiss. "Good night, my precious wife," he whispered. He walked out, closing the door after him. He stood in the kitchen, his heart pounding. Could he stay away from her tonight? "Help me, Father God," he whispered. "In myself

I don't have the strength, but in you I do."

In the bedroom Maple crept into bed and pulled the covers to her chin. She heard Hadley in the kitchen, then all was quiet. She listened to make sure he wasn't coming in. All she heard was a cricket and her pounding heart. Slowly she relaxed and finally closed her eyes. She gingerly touched a fingertip to her lips.

The next morning a fire was crackling in the stove and the boiler on the stove was full of hot water. The tub sat between the stove and the table. On the table beside the lamp she saw a stubby pencil and a torn piece of tablet paper. She picked up the paper. "I milked the cow. I must check the horses in the west pasture. Be back by noon." It was signed only with a large H.

She traced the H with an unsteady finger. He had let her sleep! She should have gotten up to make his breakfast. She knew enough to know that was a wife's job. Tomorrow she'd get up earlier.

She walked to the door and looked out at the wide blue sky and bright morning sun. Wind whirled the blades of the windmill and pushed down the prairie grass, making it look like a sea of grass. She took a deep breath. It was good to be here on such a beautiful morning. Momma wasn't here to tell her to hurry with her chores or to get out of her robe and get dressed. It felt strange.

With a laugh she walked to the bedroom to find clothes to wear today. None of her dresses suited. Maybe she could wear something of Hadley's again. She noticed the leather humpback trunk with brass trim at the foot of the bed. Maybe he had clothes in there. She unhooked the lid and lifted it. The smell of sachet drifted up. Right on top lay a blue and white gingham dress. Tiny white buttons ran in a row down the bodice of the dress and up the cuffs. "It's beautiful!" She lifted it out and held it to her. Whose dress was it? It looked new and smelled like sachet. The dress would be perfect to wear! It was pretty but serviceable. Surely Hadley wouldn't care if she wore it.

Maple took a long, relaxing bath, then dressed in her underclothes and the blue gingham. The dress nipped in at the gathered waist, then hung gracefully to just above the floor. She slipped on her high-top shoes with the low heel. She cuffed up the sleeves almost to her elbows. Now she could work in comfort.

A bucketful at a time, she emptied the tub out on the ground. She pushed the tub to the side of the kitchen. It was too heavy and awkward for her to carry outdoors. She glanced at the mantle clock on the shelf in back of the rocker. It was eleven already. She had only an hour to fix dinner. She found canned beef Momma had sent with them and a bag of potatoes. She peeled several potatoes and put them on to boil. She opened a jar of corn she'd helped Momma can last year and poured it into a pan. It was too late to make bread, but she quickly mixed up a batch of biscuits, cut them into rounds, and slipped them into the oven. Heat rushed out at her, turning her face as red as her hair. She set the table for two, then stood back and admired her work. For the first

time in her life Maple was thankful Momma had
forced her to learn to cook. When the food was
ready she pushed it to the back of the stove to stay
warm. She wrapped the biscuits in a heavy white
dishtowel to keep them warm.

Just then the door opened and Hadley walked in.
He stopped short and stared at Maple. She was
wearing the dress! The strength left his body and
his head spun.

Maple smiled at him, then the smile faded.
"What's wrong?" she asked weakly.

Hadley couldn't speak for a while. Suddenly the
words burst from him. "Take that dress off now!"

"What . . . what's wrong?"

He pointed to her and to the bedroom. "Get in
there and take off that dress!" His hand shook and
he dropped it to his side. "Go now!" He tried to
calm himself, but he couldn't. She had no right to
wear that dress.

Maple ran to the bedroom and quickly took off
the dress and folded it back in the trunk. She pulled
on a white muslin dress that didn't suit at all, but it
was the first one she grabbed. She buttoned it with
shaking fingers and tied the belt in a bow at the back
of her waist. Finally she walked to the kitchen,
her legs weak and shaky. Hadley sat at the table,
his head in his hands. In silence she dished up dinner
and set it on the table. "I'm sorry," she said. "I
didn't think it would matter if I wore it."

He lifted his haggard face. "Don't touch it
again."

"Why not?"

"I don't want to talk about it."

She'd never seen him so upset. Slowly she sat down.

He struggled to put the sight of her in the dress out of his mind. Finally he said, "I'm sorry I got so upset."

"I didn't think you'd care."

"I know."

She fingered her napkin.

He took a steadying breath. "Dinner looks good."

"Thank you."

He bowed his head and prayed a quick prayer over the food.

She watched him curiously. She wanted to ask him about the dress, but didn't dare upset him again. Instead she handed him the beef. "Did you find the horses in the west pasture?"

"Yes." He was glad for the chance to talk about something other than the dress. He spooned food onto his plate as he told her about the horses he was feeding for some ranchers who had run out of grazing land. "It makes Buck Lincoln mad. He used that land for years, but never bothered to claim it legally."

Maple swallowed a bite of potatoes. She still felt the tension in Hadley, but tried to ignore it. "Papa used land for years that wasn't really his too, but when he heard land was being sold he made sure he claimed his. He always said Lincoln was too stubborn for his own good. He thinks he's above the law."

"He sure does! My north pasture borders his place. I have cattle there and I have to check the fences regular-like. He said he'd kill any stock of mine that got on his place."

Maple frowned. "I don't like it that you have to be that close to his place. Brindle would just as soon shoot you as look at you."

"Lincoln won't let 'em kill me or I'd already be dead. He don't mind if they cripple me, though. He wants me out of here real bad." Hadley finished eating and pushed back from the table. "I got a present for you."

Maple's eyes widened. "Oh?"

"I bought it in town yesterday and hid it in the barn so you wouldn't run across it." Hadley chuckled. "You didn't happen to find it and open it, did you?"

She laughed and shook her head. She was pleased he was over his anger at her wearing the dress. It sometimes took Papa days to get over his anger. Momma never did.

Hadley started for the door. "I'll get it."

Maple jumped up. "I'll go with you."

"Can't wait, huh?" Hadley grinned as he held the door open for her.

Two dogs raced toward the house, wagging their tails.

"Where'd they come from?" Maple asked in surprise as they pressed right up against her. They were short-haired, tall, with pointed ears, and long tails. She stroked the brown one, then the black one, smiling with pleasure.

Hadley called the dogs to heel. "I had 'em over at the Smith's and picked 'em up this morning. I call 'em Pete and Repete."

Maple laughed.

"If you watch, you'll notice the brown dog always copies the black dog. They've done it since they were pups." Hadley picked up a stick and threw it across the yard. Pete raced after it, then Repete followed.

"I always wanted a dog."

"Now you have two." Hadley saw the pleased look in her eyes and wished he could keep her happy always.

Inside the barn Maple waited until her eyes become accustomed to the dimness before she followed Hadley to a stall to the left of the door. The smell of manure and freshly cut hay were strong. A cat streaked across the hard dirt-packed stall and disappeared behind a mound of hay.

Hadley opened an old wooden box with leather strap hinges and lifted out the brown bundle he'd carried from the general store yesterday. "This is for you." He held it out to her and smiled.

Hesitantly she took it. The paper crackled in her hands. "What is it?"

"Open it and see."

"You shouldn't have bought me anything."

He leaned toward her. "I'd give you the whole state of Nebraska and even Dakota Territory if I could."

She frowned and thrust the bundle back at him. "I don't want anything from you!"

He jumped back, his hands behind his back. "It's yours and I won't take it back. Takin' a present from me doesn't tie you to me more than you already are." He smiled. "Please, Maple. Take it. You'll like it."

She studied him, then looked down at the bundle. Why not take it since it meant so much to him? Besides, she was curious to see what he'd bought her. Slowly she untied the string and pulled it off. She pushed aside the brown paper. There was a blue plaid shirt and stiff dark blue levis. She looked at Hadley with a slight frown.

He laughed as he took the pants and unfolded them. "I bought clothes your size so you could ride with me when you want."

Unexpected tears stung her eyes. "Thank you," she said around the lump in her throat.

"I would've bought boots, but I saw you already had a pair."

"I do." It seemed strange to her that he even cared enough to notice.

He lifted her chin with his fingers. "Will you work with me?"

"Yes!" Maple trembled.

"Good!"

"Momma would have a fit!"

Hadley clamped a hand on Maple's shoulder. "You're at your own place now and you're your own person. You can do what you want."

She bit her lip. Was that possible?

Hadley's jaw hardened. "Our kids won't be treated like you were!"

"They sure won't!"

Hadley caught her close and swung her around with a loud whoop. "We'll be happy, Maple! That's a promise!"

She pushed against his chest and finally he let her go. She held her clothes close and ran to the house, the feel of his arms still on her.

Hadley stood in the barn door and watched her until she slipped into the house. He laughed under his breath. "My heavenly Father, thank you for givin' me the perfect wife for me."

A tiny yellow kitten mewed at Hadley's booted foot. He bent down and scooped it up. It was a little bigger than his hand. "You're a mite of a thing, aren't you? I think I'll give you to Maple for a house cat. She'll like that. Her momma would never let her have a pet even though she wanted one real bad."

In the kitchen he called, "Maple, I got another present for you." Chuckling, he hid the kitten behind his back. "It's not the state of Nebraska, but it's close."

Her cheeks flushed, she stepped from the bedroom where she'd been trying to find the courage to try on her new clothes. "I don't expect gifts, Hadley."

"I know you don't. But I got one here for you anyway."

She hung back. "What is it?"

"Guess."

She frowned. "I have no idea!"

Slowly he held his hand out to her. The kitten

mewed.

Maple gasped, then laughed with delight. "What a sweet, fluffy, yellow kitten!" She took the kitten from Hadley and held it to her cheek. "Oh, thank you!"

"It can be your house cat if you want."

"Oh, I want!"

Hadley wanted to pull Maple close and hold her forever, but he kept his hands to himself. "I'd better get back to work. I'll be home later."

"Bye." She watched him until he reached the door. "Thank you for the kitten."

"You're more than welcome." Hadley looked back at her, smiled, settled his wide-brimmed hat in place, and walked out. He had to get away before he did something he'd regret. He couldn't push her too hard or he might lose her forever.

Maple ran to the door and watched Hadley mount his sorrel gelding in one easy motion. He looked toward the house, tipped his hat, then rode away across the prairie, Pete and Repete racing after him. Maple rubbed her cheek against the kitten. "Fluffy, he is a nice man, I think."

Fluffy mewed.

Maple laughed. "So, you agree, do you? You come with me and I'll try on my new clothes." She set Fluffy on the bedroom floor, undressed, and slipped on the shirt and levis. The sleeves were the right length and the shirt hung comfortably loose on her lean body. She tucked it into the levis and tightened her belt. The levis fit snugly, but not too tight. She twisted and turned in front of the looking glass. After a few washings the pants would feel better against her skin. She smiled at her reflection, then looked closer. Why, she wasn't as ugly as before! What was different? She studied herself. Were her eyes sparkling? Was she happy? Was that the difference? She didn't seem so gaunt. Even her hair wasn't ugly. She shrugged and turned away from her reflection. She really should take off the new clothes until she was working with Hadley, but she couldn't part with them yet. After slipping on her shoes and tying them, she pulled on work gloves. "Come on, Fluffy. We have work to do."

Outdoors she dug deep holes for the rose bushes, filled the holes with water, and planted the bushes. She stood back with a pleased smile. "Once they grow big, they'll look pretty along the side of the house."

She kept busy all day, thankful for Fluffy's company. Several times she looked out across the prairie for Hadley. Just before dark she milked the cow and did the other chores. She found a hen nesting on several eggs in the last stall. It ruffled its feathers, scolded, and pecked at her.

"Go right ahead and hatch them. But don't you peck at me again!"

Maple carried the other eggs in her woven basket to the house. She changed into her yellow dress and braided her hair. She fixed fried potatoes with beef and baked a pan of cornbread. She stood at the door and watched for Hadley. Supper got cold on the stove. Her nerves tightened. She lit the lamp and waited in the rocker, Fluffy curled on her lap.

She absently rubbed her fingers over Fluffy's soft hair. Had something dreadful happened to Hadley? She heard a yap of a coyote and the screech of an owl. Near at hand a cricket chirped. A moth struck the screen door.

She thought of the newspapers Momma had packed for her to read, but she couldn't concentrate enough to read about world or state affairs or town gossip. Keene was too small to have a newspaper, so Momma subscribed to the Grand Island paper. At home Momma had quizzed her on what was in the paper to make certain she'd read it. She had enjoyed the gossip and the advertisements, but the news had bored her.

"It's important to know what's going on in the world around you," Momma often said.

The only world Maple could think about right now was what was happening to her and to Hadley.

Much later she heard the sound of pounding hooves. She leaped up, holding Fluffy close, and ran outdoors. Bright stars twinkled in the dark sky. A gentle wind blew a pleasantly cool breeze against her suddenly hot body. She caught sight of the horse and rider. "Hadley! I'm so glad you're home!" she shouted.

"It's not Hadd, Mrs. Clements." The rider stopped near her and dropped to the ground. He was a thin boy in his mid-teens. "I'm Tad Smith. We have the ranch to the west of you." He raked off his wide-brimmed hat. "Ma sent me."

Maple clutched at her throat. "Is something wrong with Hadley?"

"No. He's helpin' Pa hunt down a wildcat that's been after our calves."

Maple's blood froze. "A wildcat?"

Tad nodded. "They didn't think they'd be late, but Ma says once they start huntin' they won't quit till they get it. She said she didn't want you frettin' all alone here, so she sent me to tell you not to expect Hadd until you see him."

"Tell your mother thank you." Maple laced her icy fingers together. "Would you like to come in for a bite to eat?"

"No, thanks. I got to get right back. Ma said."

"Wait!" Maple ran inside, cut a huge piece of cornbread and ran back out. She gave it to Tad.

"Thanks." Tad swung easily into the saddle, turned the horse, and rode away at a trot.

Maple stood in the moonlight and starlight until she could no longer hear the pounding hooves. She looked at the stars. They seemed close enough to touch. Would Hadley notice them and think about them counting stars together or was he too busy hunting the wildcat?

Slowly Maple walked back inside and sank down in the rocker with Fluffy in her lap. Fluffy purred.

"Hadd's safe. He'll be home. We won't worry."

Maple leaned her head back, her ears strained to catch any sound of Hadley's horse. If she knew how to pray, she'd pray. She bit her lip and moaned.

After a long time Maple climbed into bed without undressing. She curled in a ball and fell asleep listening for Hadley's return.

CHAPTER 5

The next morning Maple slowly finished the chores and filled the boiler with water to heat for the washing. The sky was a little hazy, but she was sure it would clear off and be sunny later. She yawned. Last night had seemed like three years, not the few hours it was.

She forced herself to eat some of the left-over supper. The cornbread stuck in her throat and she washed it down with cold milk.

The sound of a wagon coming drifted through the door. She leaped up and raced outdoors, holding up the skirt of her green dimity. The wagon looked like one a medicine man or a peddler used and was painted barn red with shiny black trim. It was pulled by one black horse with a huge white circle around its left eye. Maple studied the driver. It wasn't the peddler she knew, but there was something familiar about him. He wore a big hat that had seen better days, overalls, and a plaid shirt buttoned to his throat. He spotted her and doffed his hat. She gasped. She knew him! It was Rand Rawlings! As sure as she was breathing, it was him!

With a glad cry she ran to meet the wagon. She

hadn't seen Rand since Momma had forced Papa to fire him. That was nine years ago when she was sixteen and in love with him. He had taught her how to notice details around her—the nest the meadowlarks built, the soft fluff inside the pods on cottonwood trees, the brown paper-like wrapper covering a single sand cherry, the beautiful colors of flying grasshopper's legs, the glory of a mare giving birth. Maple had wanted to learn everything Rand could teach her, but Momma said Rand was only a cowboy, not fit company for a rancher's daughter.

Rand stopped the wagon and jumped to the ground. "Maple Raines, is it really you?"

"Sure is!" She caught his hands and squeezed them. He was the same height as she was. He looked older, but happy. His curly brown hair needed to be cut. Laugh lines spread from the corners of his hazel eyes to a beginning of gray at his temples. "What brings you here?"

"I saw your place and I needed to water my horse. And myself too." His eyes softened. "Maple. I thought of you a lot. I always wondered what became of you."

She flushed. "I live here. I'm . . . married."

"You don't say! Who's the lucky guy?"

"Hadley Clements."

"I don't reckon I know him."

She led the black horse to the tank and let him drink. "Where're you heading?"

"To see Buck Lincoln."

Maple frowned. "Why?"

Rand filled the dipper with icy cold water and drank. He hung the dipper in place and rubbed a hand over his mouth. "I found a herd of stray cattle and I figured I could make a few dollars by selling them to him. Him being the big rancher he is."

"I'll buy them." The words surprised her, but the minute they were out, she knew she meant them. She nodded. "I'll take them."

Rand shook her hand and grinned. "You got yourself a deal."

"Could you get a couple of men to help you bring them here? I'll pay."

Rand settled his hat in place. "Sure can. I'll have 'em here in maybe three days. I could get 'em here sooner, but I don't dare cross Lincoln's land."

She led Rand to the bench and they sat down. "Lincoln's been trying to get Hadley to sell. He won't, of course."

"I always knew you'd marry a headstrong rancher." Rand tugged Maple's braid. "You look happy."

She didn't want to talk about that. "Come inside for a bite to eat and I'll get you some money for the cattle."

Rand walked inside and sat in the rocker and talked to Maple as she heated the left-overs for him and made a fresh pot of coffee. Nobody was ever turned away from a Nebraska home without food and rest. Even Momma kept the unwritten law although she complained at times.

A few minutes later Maple sat across the table from Rand and watched him eat while she sipped a cup of coffee. "Who are you working for now?"

Rand flushed slightly. "I quit cowboyin' a while back and only do it when my belly touches my backbone."

"Then what do you do?"

"I reckon I can tell you."

Maple leaned forward, suddenly very curious.

"I been paintin' and drawin' this Nebraska land and all that's on it."

"That's wonderful! That's what you always wanted to do."

Rand grinned with pleasure. "I didn't know if you'd recollect that."

"You were my only friend."

"But no more. You got yourself a husband. Any kids?"

Maple reddened. "I just got married." She jumped up and refilled his cup. She fixed the fire and noticed the water in the boiler was almost boiling. "Don't let Lincoln know you're bringing cattle to us or he'll make trouble for you too."

"A team of horses can't drag it from me."

A few minutes later Rand climbed on the high seat of his wagon, tipped his hat, and rode off into the prairie. Maple watched until he was out of sight. She knew he and Hadley would like each other. Maybe when Rand brought the cattle Hadley would be home and they could meet.

With a deep sigh Maple watched for Hadley. Was he safe? Slowly she walked back to the house to do the wash.

Later she hung wet clothes on the line to dry in

the hot wind while Fluffy walked around her feet.
She often glanced across the prairie to see if Hadley
was coming. Did he know she was worried about
him? Maybe he was so used to living alone he'd
never given her a thought.

She wiped her hands on the big white apron
covering her green dimity that was unsuitable for
work. As Mr. Turner's wife she would have had a
maid to do the washing. She wrinkled her nose at
the thought of being Ed Turner's wife.

In the distance she heard hoofbeats. She lifted
her head, her heart racing. Hadley was coming
home! He was safe. "Thank you, God." She gasped.
Had she prayed?

Maple watched the rider come closer. He was
riding a big palomino. It wasn't Hadley! Disap-
pointment left her weak. The big man astride the
palomino wore a white Stetson hat, a red shirt that
fit snugly across his broad shoulders, and dark
pants. A holster with a Colt in it was tied to his
muscled leg. As he drew closer she recognized him
as Buck Lincoln. She trembled and her mouth turned
bone dry. He stopped a few feet away and sat easy in
his hand-tooled black saddle trimmed in silver.

"Good morning," Maple said. Dare she run to the
house for the rifle hanging over the door?

Buck Lincoln touched the brim of his hat.
"Where's Hadd Clements?" he asked in a gravelly
voice, his steel gray eyes boring into hers.

"He'll be home soon. Can I help you?"

He slid off his horse with lithe grace in a man so
big. He walked to her side and stood with his booted

feet apart. He pulled off one leather glove and slapped it against his hand. "You tell Hadd Clements Buck Lincoln came to call."

"I know who you are," she said coldly.

His gray eyes narrowed, then he laughed. "And I know you, Maple Raines Clements. My men told me about your weddin'."

"I'm sure they did."

Lincoln chuckled, then the humor vanished from his face and iron determination took its place. "You tell that new husband of yours I'll pay him five hundred dollars over what he paid for this place. I'm not sayin' it's not already mine, mind you. I'm just willin' to make it right by him."

"He won't sell."

Lincoln narrowed his eyes into steel gray slits. "You tell him if he wants to stay healthy and if he wants his red-headed bride to stay healthy, he'd better take my offer."

The short hairs on the back of her neck stood on end, but she faced him squarely, her chin high. "Don't threaten me or Hadley! We're here to stay!"

Lincoln jabbed his finger at her. "You talk him into sellin', Red. You hear?"

She shook her head, her face as white as the cotton ball clouds up above.

He gripped her arms with large powerful hands. Fluffy spat and leaped away, its tail huge, its back arched. "You ready to die, Red?"

"You won't kill me!"

"There's no law around these parts."

"Hadley would kill you if you killed me."

Lincoln shook his head. "He don't believe in killin'." He shoved Maple back. "You tell him what I said."

She stumbled and her feet tangled in her skirts. She sprawled to the ground near the bench. Before she could move he drew his Colt and aimed it right at her. Her heart caught in her throat.

"I mean to get this place back." Lincoln pulled back the hammer, then turned the Colt and shot the little kitten.

Maple screamed and tried to get up.

Lincoln swung into the saddle and rode away at a gallop.

Maple sobbed as she untangled herself and crawled over to her dead kitten. Bile filled her mouth and she retched. She turned away, sobbing hard. Through her sobs she heard the thunder of hooves. She brushed at her eyes and jumped up. Was Lincoln coming back to shoot her? She looked toward the rider and saw it was Hadley. With a strangled cry she ran to meet him.

He leaped off his horse before it stopped and grabbed Maple tight to him. "What happened? I heard a shot."

She clung to him, sobbing against his sweaty neck. "Buck Lincoln killed Fluffy."

Hadley held Maple fiercely. He had thought he would find Maple dead. "But you're safe. Thank God! Thank God you're safe!"

She felt him tremble and thought he was crying. But that couldn't be. He couldn't care that much about her.

Finally he held her away from him and she did see his dark lashes wet with tears. Her heart jerked strangely.

Hadley pulled her close again. "We'll get you another kitten. But we could never get another Maple. I'm so glad you're all right." He rubbed his cheek against her hair. "First thing in the morning I'm takin' you home where you'll be safe."

She reared back, pushing hard against his broad chest. "I won't go home just because of this!"

Hadley looked at her in surprise. "But you don't really want to be here."

She couldn't speak for a minute. He was right, wasn't he? "But I won't let Buck Lincoln make me leave."

Hadley shook his head. "I'll take you back in the morning."

"No! No, Hadley!"

He rubbed an unsteady hand over his day-old whiskers. "Maple, I won't have you killed over my fight with Buck Lincoln."

"I'm not going."

"Oh, yes, you are!"

She knotted her fists at her sides. "I'm here and I mean to stay! I planted my roses."

"We can dig 'em up."

"My things are put away in the house."

"We can load them back again."

Her breast rose and fell. "Who'll cook for you?"

"I did just fine before you came."

"Who'll keep your hair cut?"

Hadley sprang at her and flung her over his

shoulders like a sack of grain and carried her to the house. "I'm takin' you back, so don't say another word."

The blood rushed to her head as she struggled to get free. He dropped her on the bed in a heap. She scrambled up, her eyes flashing.

"You said I could be in charge of my own life! You said that. I want to stay. I will stay!"

He opened the drawer, pulled out a handful of her clothes, and flung them to the bed.

She threw herself against him and wrapped her arms around him. "Hadd, don't make me leave."

He pried at her, but she clung tighter. "Why are you doing this?"

She didn't know herself. She just knew she couldn't go back to her other life. "Don't make me go," she whispered. She pressed her lips against his face close to his mouth. "Don't make me go. Please don't."

His will to fight her vanished. He moved his head until their lips touched. Fire leaped in his veins and he knew he could never let her leave.

Suddenly a shot rang out from out on the prairie.

Reluctantly Hadley pulled free of Maple and ran to the door with Maple close behind. A short, wiry man about thirty-five years old with a big floppy hat rode up on a brown mule. "It's Obid Smith."

Maple locked her icy fingers together as she waited beside Hadley.

"What's wrong?" Hadley called as Obid stopped the mule.

"I saw that old wildcat near them horses of

yours," Obid said with his hat in his hands.

Hadley turned to Maple. "I have to go. You keep close watch out for Lincoln or his men."

"I will."

Hadley turned back to Obid. "Obid, this is my wife, Maple. I told you about her."

Obid smiled broadly. "Glad to meet you, Maple."

"I'm pleased to meet you." Just what had Hadley told him about her? "I already met your son, Tad."

"He told me. I'll send him back again if it looks like we'll be gone too long."

"Thank you."

Hadley squeezed Maple's hand and smiled into her eyes. "Please be careful."

"You too." She'd seen what a wildcat could do to a man and she shivered.

He looked at her mouth and she was afraid he was going to kiss her again. She stepped back. He squeezed her hand, ran to his horse, and rode away with Obid.

Maple watched until they were tiny black dots on the prairie. She touched her lips and flushed scarlet.

Later she tearfully buried Fluffy. She tried to keep busy the rest of the day. Once she picked up Hadley's Bible and gently stroked the black cover. Opening the cover she read the inscription inside: *To our precious son Hadley from Pa and Ma, 1886.* She closed it and laid it back on the shelf.

After chores and supper she lit the lamp and sat

in the rocker watching out the screen door. Moths flew against the screen. A coyote barked and another answered. A cricket played its fiddle in the corner behind the stove. The moon came out bright enough to cast shadows. She blew out the lamp and sat in the rocker again, gripping the arms with both hands.

Sometime later she heard hoofbeats and she sprang out the door. Her pulse leaped. Hadley was coming and he was safe! The rider came into sight. It was Tad Smith, not Hadley. Maple's heart sank.

Tad jumped to the ground. His horse was lathered with sweat. "You got to come with me."

"Hadley?" His name tore through her throat. "Is he hurt?"

"No."

She sagged in relief.

"My pa is." Tad raked his hand across his face and couldn't speak for a while. "Hadd said you could tend him. Said you knew about healin' herbs. I was with 'em and saw the cat get him." Tad's voice broke. "Hadd said he'd get Pa home while I came for you."

A calmness settled over Maple and she turned very business-like. "I'll change and get my things." Momma had packed special healing herbs for her. "Saddle two fresh horses and I'll be right out." Maple watched Tad turn toward the barn, then she ran into the house. She changed into the levis and shirt Hadley had bought her, grabbed her bag, and ran to meet Tad. She'd hated to learn what herbs and salves to use, but Momma had insisted.

Now Maple was glad.

She mounted the sorrel and Tad quickly adjusted her stirrups. She saw the anguish on his face. "I'll do the best I can for him, Tad."

He brushed at his eyes. "He's real bad."

"Do you know how to pray?" The question shocked her.

Tad nodded. "So does my family and Hadd."

"Good."

Tad leaped into the saddle and raced back out onto the prairie.

Maple leaned low over the saddle and followed Tad. Wind whipped at her hat and billowed out the back of her shirt. The moon lit a bright path for them, making the night sky almost like day.

Several minutes later she saw a light and knew they were almost to the Smith's place. In the moonlight she made out a two-story frame house, a large barn, and several other buildings. She stopped at the house and jumped to the ground. Tad caught the reins to her mount and rode off to the barn. Maple ran up on the wide porch to the door.

Hadley flung the door wide and tugged her inside. He squeezed her hand and devoured her with his eyes. "Obid's in bad shape, but I know you'll help him. We just got here and I put him on the bed."

She dropped her hat on a peg beside the door just as a short, slight woman ran in from another room. She wore a faded calico dress that almost brushed the wooden floor.

"Maple, this is Elly, Obid's wife and Tad's ma.

Elly, Maple will help Obid." Hadley pointed toward the half-open door across the room.

"I will," Maple said softly. She felt sorry for the distressed woman.

"Thank you!" Elly blinked back tears and took a deep breath. "What do you need?"

"Clean bandages and hot water." Maple strode across the room and into the bedroom where Obid lay unconscious on the bed. Two lamps lit the room enough for her to see the deep scratches across his chest and arms. She trembled. She'd taken care of men in as bad a shape as Obid, but never without Momma's help.

Elly set the basin of hot water on a table beside the bed. "Tell me what to do."

"I'll soak off the shirt first. You can help peel it away from his wounds." The shirt was in bloody ribbons. Not a scratch was on his legs or his back. His face had only one long scratch that wasn't very deep. Carefully Maple sponged around the wounds until the shirt came loose. Together she and Elly pulled the shirt away. Carefully Maple cleaned the wounds, sewed the deep scratches shut, caked her mixture of herbs over them, then gently bandaged them. She smiled tiredly at Elly. "He's going to be just fine."

"Thank God!" Elly covered her face and sobbed.

Maple stood awkwardly beside her. "I'll leave you alone with him. He's asleep now and not unconscious. Sleep's good for him."

Elly smiled weakly and sank to a chair beside the bed.

Maple walked out of the bedroom and closed the door softly. She felt almost too tired to walk.

Tad sprang to her side. "How's Pa?"

"He's fine. It'll take a few days, but he'll be up and around before you know it."

Tad turned away to hide his tears.

Hadley stepped forward, a baby against his shoulder. The sight stirred a yearning inside Maple she had never experienced before. Hadley clamped a hand on Tad's shoulder. "Get to bed, Tad. You'll have to take care of things alone for a while."

Tad nodded, mumbled goodnight and walked to a narrow flight of stairs. His steps dragged as he climbed.

Hadley took Maple's arm and led her to a rocking chair near the stone fireplace. "You look ready to collapse. Sit and rest."

She sank to the chair thankfully. "His wounds are deep, but he really will make it."

"Good." Hadley smiled as he sank down on a chair beside her.

"Elly is right done in."

"I told her I'd tend baby Obid for her."

Maple smiled. "You look like you know how."

"I took care of my share at home."

"Do they have just the two boys?"

Hadley shook his head. "Three girls between the two boys. Sara, Amy, and Jane. It's a fine family."

"And they almost lost their papa." Maple sighed heavily. "Did you get the wildcat?"

"Yes. I had to shoot while it was on Obid."

Hadley shuddered. "It was mauling him right before my eyes. I felt helpless."

"I'm glad you weren't hurt."

"Me too." Hadley shifted the baby in his arms. "He's asleep. I'll put him back to bed." He carried him to a wooden cradle and carefully laid him on his stomach. He smiled down at him, then spread a light cover over him.

Maple blinked back tears. Had Papa ever put her to sleep when she was a baby? Or was he always too busy the way he had been while she was growing up? She had gone into his world because he never seemed to have time to come into hers.

Hadley walked back to Maple and took her hand. "I'm going home now."

"I'll check Obid and be right with you."

Hadley shook his head. "You should stay here to tend Obid. Elly would feel better, I know."

Maple sighed and nodded. His hands felt rough and warm against hers. "It'll only be a couple of days."

Hadley pulled her close and held her tightly. She pushed against him until finally he let her go.

"I'll come get you. I don't want you ridin' alone with what Lincoln just pulled."

"Don't forget to water the rose bushes."

He grinned. "You sound like a regular wife."

She ducked her head and flushed.

He tipped up her chin and kissed her before she could stop him, then strode out the door.

She sat back in the rocker, her hand at her heart.

"He's a fine man," Elly said as she walked to the

raised hearth and sat down.

Maple nodded. He was a fine man—a man she could respect!

"He's like an uncle to our kids and a brother to Obid and me." Elly pressed her skirts over her knees. Strands of hair hung over her forehead. She looked ready to topple with fatigue. "He told us about the weddin'. He said he kind of forced you to stay with him."

Flushing, Maple nodded. "But now that he wants me to leave because of Buck Lincoln, I don't want to."

Elly grinned. "We're hard to understand, we women. I search my heart many a time to see why I do and say certain things. Sometimes I find I'm keeping my true feelings a secret even from myself."

"I know what you mean."

"I was fourteen and Obid eighteen when we got married and moved here. We had six kids—five lived." Elly's lip trembled as she pushed back her curly brown hair with a work-roughened hand. "I love Obid, but, Maple, I yearn to talk to another woman! I was so glad when Hadd said he brought home a wife! I couldn't wait to get to know you! I need to talk to another woman! To you!"

Maple leaned forward. "I don't even know if I'm a woman yet. I'm twenty-five, but I've lived my whole live with Momma telling me what to do and how to act. I'm findin' it hard to know how to act on my own."

"Ask the Lord to help you. That's what I always do."

Maple laced her fingers together. "Elly, I never prayed. I don't know how."

Elly smiled gently. "It's talkin' with God. You do know Jesus as your personal Lord and Savior, don't you?"

Maple nodded.

"He's your friend and God is your Father. Talk to 'em that way."

"It seems too easy. I thought it was real hard."

Elly shrugged.

For the next three days Elly talked non-stop. Maple enjoyed listening to her. Elly showed her how to study the Bible. Maple learned quickly, eager to remember all she could. She watched Elly treat Obid with love and respect. They laughed and talked together and even played jokes on each other. Elly talked and played with the kids and taught them how to work and even how to play fairly. Maple learned how a wife and mother really was to her family. It was a different picture than she'd seen growing up.

On the afternoon of the third day Maple said, "Elly, Obid is up and about. It's time for me to go home."

Elly frowned down at the bread dough she was kneading. Finally she looked up. "Hadd said to keep you here until he comes for you."

Maple set her coffee cup down with a bang. "He thinks it's too dangerous for me at home. Elly, does Obid send you away every time it gets dangerous here?"

Elly laughed and shook her head. "I'll tell Tad to saddle the horses. He'll ride with you most of the way. I don't want Hadd tongue lashin' Tad for doin' what's right."

Maple chuckled. "I'll get my things."

"You'll come visit soon, won't you?"

"Yes! And you come see me."

"I will." Elly's eyes filled with tears. "You don't know how good it's been havin' you here to talk to." She dusted flour off her hands and hugged Maple.

"I've learned a lot from you, Elly. I'm glad we're friends. I haven't had a friend for years." Maple suddenly remembered Rand Rawlings and the cattle deal she'd made with him. Indeed she had to get home before Rand came. She kissed Elly's soft cheek. "I'll be back. You can count on it."

"I'll be prayin' for you. And you keep prayin' for us."

"I will."

Several minutes later she rode across the prairie with Tad. Near Hadd's place she told Tad goodbye and rode the rest of the way alone. The sky was summer blue and the wind warm. Tears pricked her eyes as she saw the house and barn. She was home!

Would Hadley want her back? She lifted her chin stubbornly. This was her home and she was here to stay!

Pete and Repete barked and ran to meet her, wagging their tails. Horses milled about in the corral and a few hens scratched in the dirt near the woodshed. There weren't extra cattle so she knew

Rand hadn't come yet.

Hadley stepped from the barn, a rifle in his hand. The sight of Maple sent his pulse leaping, then he scowled angrily. Elly shouldn't have sent her home yet. It was too dangerous.

Maple stopped her horse and dropped to the ground, her eyes on Hadley. She could see he was upset. She pulled off her hat and dusted herself. "Howdy."

"You were supposed to stay with Elly."

She put her hat on, then pushed it off and let it dangle down her back. "Obid is well. I'm not needed."

"You're goin' right back!"

She lifted her chin and stepped toward him. "Oh, no, I'm not!"

"Then you're goin' home to your momma."

Maple stepped closer to Hadley. "Obid doesn't send Elly packing when danger comes. And you can't send me away!"

Hadley reached for her. "I'll hogtie you and throw you over the saddle if I have to."

She jumped away. "You wouldn't dare!"

"I am a man of my word," he said gruffly.

She could tell he meant it. She sagged in defeat. "I thought you wanted me here," she said in a tiny voice.

A muscle jumped in his jaw. "I don't."

"You don't?"

He saw the anguish in her eyes, but couldn't take back the words. Her life was too important to waste! "Get ready. We're leavin' within the hour."

With a strangled sob she ran to the house to pack. She'd go back to Momma and once again be a child in a woman's body. She'd forget all that Elly had taught her.

With her lips pressed tightly together and a sob caught in her throat Maple flipped up the trunk lid to grab out her crinoline. She stared down at the obnoxious blue gingham dress that Hadley had forbidden her to wear. A sharp pain shot through her. Who did the dress belong to? Why wouldn't Hadley explain what it meant to him and why it was there?

Impatiently she jerked out her crinoline and slammed the trunk closed. How she wanted to grab the dress and stuff it in the stove to burn to ashes! She reached to lift the trunk lid again. She would burn the dress and she would tell Hadley she never wanted to see him again!

CHAPTER 6

A tear ran down Maple's flushed cheek and she dropped her hand at her side. She couldn't burn the dress. It wouldn't be right no matter why Hadley kept it hidden away.

Just then Pete and Repete barked their special bark that meant someone was coming. Maple froze, listening intently. Was it Buck Lincoln coming back to kill them?

With a strangled cry Maple ran to the kitchen. Her boots sounded loud on the plank floor. Her levis felt hot against her long legs. She lifted the rifle off the pegs above the door. Where was Hadley? She stepped outdoors, the rifle at her side. Warm wind blew loose strands of hair against her face. She looked around for Hadley, but didn't dare shout to him in case he was hiding until he saw who was coming. As she watched, a black horse and a black buggy trimmed with narrow red stripes and a black canvas top drove into the yard. She gasped. Ed Turner was driving the buggy and a woman sat primly beside him. Maple ducked inside and hung the rifle in place, then stepped back out, tucking her shirt securely into the waist of her levis. She saw

Hadley in the door of the barn, the dogs on either side of him. His hat was pulled down on his forehead. His gray shirt was buttoned to his chin and tucked in at his lean hips. He didn't make a move to greet Ed Turner.

Ed stopped the buggy near the bench and climbed out. The buggy swayed under his weight. He wore a gray bowler, a dark suit, white shirt and collar, and blue dotted tie. He helped the woman to the ground. She was short with golden brown hair hanging to her shoulders below her hat. Her dark green traveling dress molded her figure and nipped in at her tiny waist. Maple frowned thoughtfully. Who was the woman and why had Ed Turner brought her here?

Ed looked toward the house and Maple. His brows shot up at the sight of her wearing men's clothes. He turned toward the barn and doffed his hat at Hadley.

Hadley forced back his anger at seeing Maple's intended groom on his place. He walked toward Ed and the woman. There was something familiar about her, but Hadley couldn't place her.

Maple hurried toward the buggy. She didn't want to speak to Ed Turner, but she couldn't be rude. She joined Hadley and they stood together facing Ed and the woman who was studying Hadley and smiling happily.

Ed cleared his throat. "I brought you a visitor, Clements. Lucy Everett. From St. Louis."

Hadley fell back a step, his face ashen.

Maple pressed her fingers over her mouth.

Hadley's mail-order bride! But how could she be here?

Lucy stepped up to Hadley. She looked at Maple, then back at Hadley. She held out her small, gloved hand. "Hello, Hadd." Her dark brown eyes were full of emotion. "Please don't be angry that I came now. I couldn't wait any longer. I truly couldn't!"

Hadley pulled off his hat as he took Lucy's hand in a quick shake. Finally he turned to Ed. "Didn't you tell her?"

"I couldn't!" Ed wiped sweat from his round face with a large white handkerchief.

"Tell me what, Ed?"

Maple's mouth dropped open. Lucy Everett called Mr. Turner Ed!

Ed patted Lucy's arm. "Lucy, my dear, I . . . thought Hadley Clements should tell you face to face."

Hadley looked helplessly from Lucy to Maple. A muscle jumped in his jaw. He moved closer to Maple's side. "I'm sure sorry about this, Lucy." Hadley couldn't continue.

"About what?"

"I'm already . . . married. To Maple."

Maple flushed with guilt. She knew she had no reason to feel guilty, but she couldn't help it at the devastated look on Lucy Everett's face.

Hadley motioned to Maple, then let his hand fall to his side. How he wished this situation had never arisen! "My wife, Maple."

Lucy gasped, her hand fluttering at her heart. Her legs buckled and she started to fall, but Ed caught her and held her close to him.

"Now look what you've done, Clements! The girl is delicate and sensitive."

Maple stepped forward. "Get her inside out of the sun."

Hadley reached for her, but Ed pushed him aside.

Lucy leaned heavily on Ed as she walked with him into the house. She sank down on the rocking chair and leaned her head back.

Hadley stood helplessly at the door. He watched Maple fill a glass with water. Was she as calm as she seemed?

Ed untied Lucy's hat and lifted it from her head, then carefully eased off her gloves. He dropped them to the floor beside the rocker.

"Here's a drink of water for her," Maple said, handing Ed a glass of water. She couldn't believe Ed Turner was actually waiting on Lucy. It wasn't like him to tend others.

He took the water without acknowledging Maple's presence and helped Lucy sip from the glass.

Hadley paced the room with a frown. He stopped beside Maple and tried to speak, but no words came out. He walked to the rocker, then whirled around and walked to the cold stove. He cleared his throat. "I don't know how this happened. I was goin' to send her a letter the next time I got to town."

"It's too late to think of that now," Ed said coldly.

"I know it's too late! But that's what I planned." Hadley wanted to toss Ed from the house and tell him never to return.

Lucy sighed. "Don't fight," she whispered. "I don't want to be a burden. I'll go back to town with you, Ed." She tried to stand but fell back weakly.

Ed pulled a chair close and sat beside her. "Lucy, please just relax. We'll think of something." He scowled at Hadley. "She used all her money to come from St. Louis. You know there are no jobs in Keene. And she can't be left on her own."

Hadley spread his hands wide. "I don't know what to say."

Lucy sat up straight and looked very determined. "I don't want any of you to worry about me. I'll take care of myself."

Maple could tell Lucy was serious. She hadn't come to make trouble for any of them.

"But you don't have any money," Ed said.

"I'll manage!" Lucy jumped up, swayed, and almost fell. Ed caught her and eased her down again.

"When was the last time you ate, Lucy?" Maple asked gently.

Lucy bit her lip. "I don't remember."

Ed frowned. "I thought you ate before we left town."

"I had no money."

Ed groaned. "You should've told me you hadn't eaten."

Lucy eyed him squarely. "I'm not a beggar!"

"I'll make you something." Maple turned and caught a surprised look on Hadley's face. She gave him a challenging stare and he shrugged. Did he expect her to turn Lucy out?

"I know this situation is hard on you," Lucy

said, smiling weakly at Maple.

Maple shot Hadley a knowing look then turned back to Lucy. "We'll sort it all out." Maple sliced a thick slice of bread and spread it with fresh butter and honey. She filled a glass with milk and set them on the table. "Eat this while I make dinner."

"Thank you, Mrs. Clements."

Maple's heart jerked strangely. It seemed funny to be called Mrs. Clements. "Please, call me Maple."

Lucy looked pleased. "I will! And you call me Lucy."

They smiled at each other and suddenly Maple felt as if they could be friends, given a chance.

Hadley shook his head. What was to become of all of them? The whole thing was awkward, yet Maple was handling it easily.

Ed held Lucy's arm and walked her to the table. He sat her down and turned to Hadley. "I want to talk to you in private." From his face and stance he looked ready to fight. "Shall we step outdoors?"

Hadley nodded. "It's late, Turner. You might as well plan to spend the night. I'll unhitch your horse."

"You're probably right."

They walked out and Maple breathed a sigh of relief. The tension had been too high in the room. Now she could think and plan. She already knew she would not return to town with Ed Turner. She shook the ashes down in the stove and started the fire again with some kindling.

Lucy swallowed the last bite of her sandwich

and the last swallow of her milk, then daintily wiped her mouth with a white napkin. "I'm sorry for all the trouble I've caused you."

"Don't worry about it." Maple cut into a potato with a sharp paring knife. "I wish Mr. Turner had told you the truth to save you a trip out here."

Lucy blinked back tears. "I should have known things wouldn't work out the way I dreamed."

"Can't you go back to St. Louis?"

"Never! I will never go back!"

"Oh?" Maple wanted to hear more, but she knew it was wrong to pry. She finished the potatoes and put them on to fry.

Lucy's dark eyes flashed. "I'd like to tell you my story. May I?"

Maple nodded.

Lucy brushed back a strand of golden brown hair. "I ran away! Do you think that's terrible?"

"Not at all! I know there are reasons a person runs away, even when you're an adult."

"You do understand!" Lucy took a deep breath. "I lived with my aunt. She worked me from morning 'til night without let-up, without pay, and then mocked me because I'm a poor relation." Lucy wrapped her arms across her breast and moaned. "She wouldn't let me go to church or even give me time to read my Bible and pray. I'd try to read before I went to sleep at night, but I couldn't stay awake. But I would quote a Scripture to myself and fall asleep doing it."

Maple thought of the times she could have read her Bible and prayed, but it had never occurred to her to do it.

Lucy pushed back her hair with a trembling hand. "And then she said I couldn't come west to marry Hadley Clements. She was furious when she learned I'd answered his ad. She said I had to marry a rich old man who had already had five wives! I would have been his slave!"

Maple's heart went out to Lucy. "I'm glad you ran away!"

"Me too." Lucy dabbed at her tears with her napkin.

"You're a brave girl."

"Not really. It took all the courage I had to answer Hadley's ad. After he wrote, it was easier. He seemed genuine and I knew I could be happy married to him." She flushed. "I'm sorry."

"It's not your fault." Maple sat across from Lucy and leaned forward. "We'll have to think of a way to help you."

"It's not your problem."

"I'm married to the man you were promised to. I am a little responsible." Maple couldn't bring herself to tell how she'd come to marry Hadley. "My folks have room in their house for you, but I don't think you'd want to stay with them. Momma is . . . somewhat like your aunt was."

"God will provide."

"I have a little money. Enough to take you to Omaha or even Denver."

"I won't take your money." Lucy carefully stood. "I believe I can help now. Tell me what to do."

"Just sit down and rest."

"No! I'll set the table."

Maple saw the stubborn set to Lucy's jaw and told her where to find everything for the table while she mixed up a batch of biscuits and cut them in rounds. After testing the oven's heat by putting her hand in for an instant, Maple stuck them in the oven. She opened a jar of beef and poured it into a cast iron skillet. Smells of frying meat and frying potatoes filled the kitchen.

Lucy finished setting the table and sat down again. "Hadd told me about the trouble he's having with Buck Lincoln. Is it still going on?"

"Yes. Hadley wants me to leave until it's settled, but I said I wouldn't. He'll probably try to make me go with you and Mr. Turner tomorrow."

Lucy shrugged and spread her hands wide. "Just don't go."

Maple sank to a chair. "I'm not that strong."

"You'll find a way." Suddenly Lucy giggled. "Ride out with us, but get out when we round the first hill, and walk back."

Maple laughed. "I should do it!"

Lucy reached across and squeezed Maple's hand. "I guess I'm thinking about myself and how I wish I'd walked out on my aunt years ago. But I didn't have the courage. It takes courage to take your life into your own hands and live it the way you want."

Maple nodded. "You're right." She fingered the salt shaker. "I don't know if I have that courage."

"With God's help you do."

"That's right!" Maple jumped up and squared

her shoulders. "I belong right here with my husband!"

Lucy nodded. "Yes, you do! Even though he was supposed to be *my* husband."

They looked at each other and burst into giggles.

Several minutes later Maple called Hadley and Ed Turner in for dinner. She could tell the men had been in a heated conversation. She wanted to ask about it, but didn't. She sat at the table and bowed her head while Hadley prayed, then in silence they started to eat.

"I hope you men weren't fighting about what to do with me," Lucy said as she spooned green beans on her plate.

Hadley shrugged.

"He has this crazy idea," Ed said gruffly.

Maple gripped her fork. She didn't like the sound of that.

"What is it?" Lucy asked, her brow cocked.

"I want Ed to ride with me to see Buck Lincoln in the morning," Hadley said. "I want a witness when I tell him I won't sell no matter what."

"And I want Hadley to go see Buck Lincoln and tell him he'll sell out," Ed said sharply.

"No!" Maple snapped, shaking her head.

"We're goin' to tell Lincoln to leave us alone," Hadley said in a voice that indicated that was the end of the discussion.

"Then I think Buck will kill us both," Ed said, dabbing sweat off his forehead.

"He won't." Hadley lifted a bit of beef to his mouth. He didn't want any more arguing. "We'll leave at dawn."

"I don't like it a bit," Ed snapped.

"Neither do I," Maple said, frowning. "What if Lincoln does hurt you?"

"I'm goin', Maple. That's that!" Hadley looked down at his plate so he wouldn't have to see the pain in Maple's eyes from his gruff answer.

That night with Pete and Repete at her feet Maple sat on the bench and looked up at the stars. She and Lucy were going to share the bed while Hadley and Mr. Turner slept on pallets on the kitchen floor. Lucy and Mr. Turner were saying goodnight and Hadley was still in the barn.

Slowly Hadley walked from the barn. He didn't want to talk to Maple, but he couldn't ignore her. Reluctantly he sat on the bench. "I am sorry about Lucy comin' here."

"I know you are." Maple locked her fingers together in her lap. "I want you to know I'm not leaving here no matter what happens at Buck Lincoln's tomorrow."

Hadley gritted his teeth and couldn't speak for a while. "You are so stubborn!"

"I just wanted you to know."

"I already made plans with Turner to take you back with him and Lucy."

Maple's muscles tightened. "Now who's being stubborn?"

"If you want to come back once this is settled with Lincoln, you can."

"I'm *not* leaving."

Hadley leaped up and jerked Maple with him.

"What's wrong with you, woman? Can't you let me take care of you?"

She tried to pull free, but his fingers bit into her upper arms. "I tried to make you leave me at home, but you wouldn't. Now you're stuck with me."

Hadley growled deep in his throat, dropped his hands, and strode away.

Maple watched Hadley walk into the waving prairie grass, his dogs beside him. She sank back on the bench and bowed her head.

The next morning Maple stood in the yard with Lucy and watched Hadley mount his sorrel and Ed climb in his buggy and ride away. They said they would try to be back by noon, but not to plan on them until they saw them.

Lucy sighed heavily. "Is life ever easy?"

"It sure doesn't seem like it." Maple watched for Hadley to turn and wave, but he didn't. She felt tears deep inside.

Lucy patted Pete and Repete, then walked slowly toward the house. "I couldn't survive without God's help and strength."

Maple's heart jumped in excitement. She had forgotten God was indeed her help and strength.

At the kitchen table over a cup of coffee, Maple said, "How old are you, Lucy?"

Lucy wrinkled her small nose. "Twenty-eight!"

"You look younger."

"Thanks. I feel older. I lived with Aunt Pearl since I was ten." Lucy suddenly burst into tears. "Maple, I can't go back to her! I really can't!"

"You don't have to. Find a husband and stay here in Nebraska."

Lucy dried her eyes and shuddered. "I won't marry a man unless I love him! I could get into a worse mess than with Aunt Pearl if I married a man just for convenience. I've seen how some men treat their wives." Lucy nervously ran her tongue over her lips. "How does Hadd treat you?"

"He's a kind man. But he is stubborn and he wants me to leave until this thing with Lincoln is settled."

"Ed Turner seems nice."

Maple frowned. "He's a stuffed shirt!"

"That's only a show. Inside he's soft and gentle. And quite uncertain of himself."

"Would you want to marry him?"

Lucy shrugged. "I don't know. I might. But only if I love him and he loves me."

Maple couldn't imagine Ed Turner loving anyone but himself, but she didn't say so.

Later Maple heard Pete and Repete bark. Someone was coming. With Lucy close behind her, Maple stepped outdoors and stopped in surprise. Brindle and his men walked toward them. They looked as dirty and unkempt as they had at the wedding. Their horses stood near the barn. Maple's heart dropped to her feet. "Buck Lincoln's men," she whispered to Lucy.

"We meet again, Red," Brindle said with a gruff laugh as he tucked his thumbs in his vest sleeves. His teeth were brown with tobacco stains. "We came to see Hadd Clements. Tell him to git out here.

We came to call on you newlyweds." He laughed and slapped his leg.

The other men chuckled and Banty said with a wicked grin, "Newlyweds."

"Git yer groom out here," Brindle said again.

Maple stiffened. "He's not here."

"I'll be horsewhipped!" Brindle looked at his men. "Search the place and see."

"He isn't here!" Maple cried.

Brindle dropped down on the bench and crossed his arms. "We'll wait."

The men scattered, one looking in the house and the others in the other buildings.

"And who's this good lookin' gal?" Brindle winked at Lucy.

"I'm Lucy Everett."

"Lucy Everett." Brindle looked her up and down.

Lucy flushed and turned away from him.

Maple heard a meadowlark warble and a hawk screech in the sky. Over the sounds of the men shouting back and forth to each other she strained to hear Hadley and Ed returning. Were the men toying with her, knowing Hadley and Ed were with Buck Lincoln—maybe even his prisoners?

"Me an' the boys are sure hungry." Brindle rubbed his flat stomach. He waited until the men were beside him. "Breakfast was hours ago. You two ladies fix us up some grub."

Maple nodded. Frantically she glanced around for Hadley. Her gaze fell on the fruit trees. Suddenly she remembered the toadstools she saw grow-

ing near the trees just this morning. Those toadstools would work to get rid of Brindle and his
men!

"I have some mushrooms to pick first over by
the fruit trees. To go in the stew." Had her trembling voice made Brindle suspicious?

"The boys'll be watchin' you close so don't try
to run off." Brindle laid down on the grass and
covered his face with his hat.

Maple caught Lucy's arm and pulled her along
across the yard to the fruit trees. She lifted the tail
of her apron, picked the toadstools, and put them in
her apron.

Lucy looked at Maple strangely. "Why are you
doing this? Why should you bother picking mushrooms for them?"

"They're toadstools," Maple whispered.
"They're poison."

Lucy gasped.

"So, don't eat a bite even if they tell you to."

"Are you going to kill them?" Lucy whispered
in horror.

"No. But they'll get real sick and wish they
were dead." Maple dropped the last one into her
apron. "Don't do or say anything to give it away."

"I won't." Lucy shivered.

In the house Lucy washed the toadstools and
Maple sliced them into pieces. She fried them, then
added them to the stew she'd started earlier.

Suddenly someone outdoors shouted. Maple ran
to the door with Lucy close behind.

"Look who we found," Banty said, pushing Ed

Turner forward.

"What's the meaning of this?" Ed's face was brick-red as he glared at Brindle.

Lucy clutched Maple's arm. "They're going to hurt him."

"Shhh!" Maple peered around for Hadley. Where was he? A trembling started deep inside her and she leaned against the doorway to keep from falling. Had Buck Lincoln killed Hadley?

Brindle pushed his large hand against Ed's chest. "State your business, then git!"

"I came to take the women to town."

"You can't take 'em!"

Maple bit her lip and Lucy groaned.

Ed wiped his hand across his sweaty face. "I just got back from seein' Buck Lincoln. He won't like it that you boys are here."

"We came for Hadd Clements and we ain't leavin' 'til we git him." Brindle shoved Ed toward the house. "You git inside and we'll all wait for the scarecrow."

Ed stumbled, but caught himself before he fell. He walked past Maple and stopped beside Lucy. "You all right?"

She barely nodded.

"What about Hadley?" Maple whispered.

"Yah, what about him?" Brindle asked as he walked inside. He pulled his Colt and aimed it at Ed. "Tell me where he is right now."

"Tell him!" Lucy cried.

Maple gripped the back of a chair.

Ed frowned. "It's no big secret. He went to the

Smith place to help hay. He sent me to take the women to town."

"He'll have to come home sometime." Brindle turned a chair around and straddled it. "Sit down, Turner. Let the ladies put dinner on." He sniffed deeply. "It smells mighty good."

Lucy shot a look at Maple and she frowned a warning. Maple knew Lucy wanted to tell Ed not to eat, but she couldn't do anything to make Brindle suspicious.

Brindle looked toward the door with a scowl. "It's nerve rackin' just waitin' around."

Maple knotted her fists and glared at him. "Then leave! We're not stopping you!"

"You'd like to get rid of us, wouldn't you, Red?"

"Yes!"

Lucy plucked at Maple's arm. "Maple. Don't."

Maple shrugged her off and shook her finger at Brindle. "You have better things to do than scare helpless people off their own land."

"Windy, ain't you? How is it you ain't blowed Scarecrow away? A wife like you is enough to send anyone packin'."

"Leave her alone!" Lucy slapped Brindle's arm. "She's upset."

Brindle leaped to his feet and lifted Lucy high in his arms.

Her feet dangling in the air, Lucy squealed and tried to squirm free.

"You're a feisty little hen. Mighty pretty too."

Ed jumped up and reached for Lucy. "Take your hands off her!"

"So you can have her?" Brindle laughed and shoved Lucy at Ed. "She's yours, banker man. Keep her quiet!"

Ed gripped Lucy's arms and pushed his face close to hers. "Don't do or say anything more. Hear me?"

She nodded, her face white.

Maple pulled the biscuits out of the oven. "Dinner's ready. Call in the men." Her voice sounded strained to her own ears and she wondered if Brindle noticed. Heat rose around her. The smell of the stew sickened her even though it didn't smell any different than her ordinary stew. Her hands shaking, she dished stew into thick china bowls for the men.

Lucy filled heavy white mugs with coffee.

One man stayed outdoors on watch while the others trooped in, smelling like sweat and horses. They grabbed bowls of stew, biscuits, and coffee, then sat or leaned here and there around the room. Maple watched them through her red lashes.

"Get the banker man a bowl of stew," Brindle said as he took a large bite.

Maple hesitated, then handed him a bowl. "I'll take the man on guard a bowl too."

"You stay right here. Montana, take that bowl out to Sam."

Montana took the bowl and slammed the screen door behind him.

Ed sat at the table and slowly dipped his spoon into the stew.

Maple held her breath. Suddenly the room felt twenty degrees hotter than it really was.

Lucy leaped at Ed and slapped the spoon from his hand. It clattered to the table, sending stew flying. "How dare you sit with the enemy and eat? What kind of man are you? A coward? And I thought you were so wonderful!"

Maple bit back a nervous laugh.

Ed's face turned brick-red as he stared at Lucy. "Lucy! You struck me!"

Brindle laughed and slapped his leg. "She's little and she's feisty!"

Lucy jabbed Ed again. "If you eat even one bite with these men, I'll never speak to you again."

"Close your mouth, woman!" Ed snapped.

"You tell her!" Brindle pounded Ed on the back. "You can't let no woman make you look bad in front of nobody."

Maple wanted to stop Lucy from going too far, but she didn't know what to do. She watched the men wolf down their stew and quickly refilled their bowls until the stew was gone.

Ed started to take another bite.

Lucy yanked Ed's tie. "And I thought you were a real man! I even thought I could care about you!"

"I didn't ask you to," Ed said coldly.

"I certainly couldn't if you take sides with these men." Lucy once again slapped the spoon from Ed's hand.

Brindle laughed, then burped loudly. He burped again and the men guffawed.

Maple hid a smile. One of the first symptoms was burping. Others were sweating profusely, vomiting, saliva running from the corner of the mouth, and severe stomach cramps.

Brindle groaned and clutched his stomach. Bending double, he reeled out the door and collapsed in the yard. The others clumped out the door after him, burping and swearing.

Ed frowned, then turned to Maple and Lucy. "What's going on here?"

"Toadstools," Lucy whispered.

Ed looked at Lucy in shock, down at his bowl, and over at Maple.

"So that's why you wouldn't let me eat it."

Lucy grinned and nodded.

"In a few minutes they'll be too weak to resist us, so we'll get their guns, then load them in the wagon." Maple laughed grimly. "We'll take them directly to Buck Lincoln with the message that he can't run us off our place."

Lucy giggled. "I've had more excitement since coming west than I've had all my life."

Maple ran outdoors and started collecting the guns from the men. Three men were out cold and the others were too sick to move.

As she started for the barn to get the wagon, she heard the sound of cattle coming and cowboys whistling and shouting. A cloud of dust drifted over a low hill. Rand Rawlings was bringing in the strays.

Maple threw back her head and laughed. The timing was perfect. Rand would know what to do with Brindle and his men. Rand might even know what to do about Lucy.

CHAPTER 7

Maple stood in the yard with Ed and Lucy and watched the bawling cattle coming closer. A dust cloud followed them. "A cowboy I know is bringing cattle for me to buy."

"For *you* to buy?" Ed asked with his brow raised.

Maple nodded.

"Hadd won't like it." He rubbed his balding head. "You're too bold for a woman, Maple. Too bold indeed."

"I don't think so," Lucy said, smiling at Maple. "We both should be bold and daring from now on."

"If we can." Maple brushed her hands down her apron. She turned to Ed. She wanted something settled before Rand reached them. "Now tell me where Hadley is."

"After we talked to Buck Lincoln, I came here and Hadd rode on to the Smith's. I know he didn't want another fight with you, Maple."

"I'm not going with you no matter what you say," Maple said firmly. "With Lincoln's men sick for a while and Rand here to help, there's no reason to leave."

"What about you, Lucy?" Ed asked.

"I don't rightly know." Lucy patted her flushed cheeks. "I know something will turn up. It has to!"

Maple touched Lucy's arm. "You're welcome to stay here until you decide what you're going to do."

"What?" Ed cried.

"Thank you!" Lucy squeezed Maple's hand, then turned to Ed. "I'd like you to come and visit me."

"It's a ways out here. I'd like you to go to town with me."

"No, Ed. It wouldn't look right."

Ed nodded. "You're right, of course."

Maple saw the look that passed between them and wondered if Ed would have a bride and Lucy a groom after all. Maple wrinkled her nose. Lucy deserved better than Ed.

"I have to get back to the bank. I'll try to come next week." Ed took Lucy's hand in his. "Buck Lincoln will be on a rampage after he learns what happened today. Be on guard."

"Are you leaving now?" Lucy asked.

Ed nodded. "I have work piling up."

"Don't you want to stay until the cattle are in?" Maple asked.

"I can't take the time." Ed settled his bowler in place. "I put your trunk inside, Lucy."

"I know. Thank you."

"Keep careful watch out for Buck Lincoln."

"We will." Lucy walked Ed to the buggy. "Don't get so busy that you forget about me."

"I won't." Ed smiled and drove away.

Maple glanced at Brindle and his men tied up on the ground in the shade of the cottonwood. They were either unconscious or asleep. They certainly weren't going anywhere until she wanted them to. Slowly she walked to the bench and sat down. She shielded her eyes against the sun and looked across the prairie. What would Hadley do when he came home and found both her and Lucy, Lincoln's men, and a herd of strays? This was a much bolder move than shaving his beard and cutting his hair. Asking Lucy to stay was the worst though.

Maple bit her lip. What if Hadley realized he was in love with Lucy? Maple's stomach knotted. Had she made a big mistake in having Lucy stay?

Lucy waved to Ed again, then joined Maple on the bench. "I've never seen a cattle drive." Lucy watched the cattle coming closer. "They're sure noisy."

"Can you ride, Lucy?"

"No. Well, some."

Maple jumped up, her hands clasped at her throat. "We could ride out and meet the herd."

"I'd love to, but I really can't ride well enough."

Maple looked longingly toward the cattle.

"But you go ahead. I'll start supper."

Maple grinned. "We'll make a good team, Lucy."

Lucy laughed and nodded. "We sure will! I do want to learn to ride better." She lowered her voice. "I read a few dime novels about cowboys before Aunt Pearl caught me. I want to meet a real cowboy."

"You will when Rand gets here."

A few minutes later Maple rode out to meet Rand. She had changed into her levis and felt right at home in the saddle. She tied a big red neckerchief around her neck to pull up over her mouth and nose as soon as she was close to the cattle. She saw two men she didn't recognize riding point, so she kept on until she found Rand to the back and side of the herd. She waved to him and he waved his hat high over his head. The cattle looked fat and healthy and were a cross between range cattle and Herefords. Most of them were young stock. A dark red short-horn bull with short legs, and a huge, sturdy body stayed at the side of the herd. She knew someone had paid a fortune for the shorthorn. If it wasn't branded, she'd slap Hadley's brand on it and call it his.

Rand stopped his horse and slapped dust off himself. He rode the same horse that had pulled his wagon.

"Glad to see you, Rand!" Maple reined in beside him and smiled happily. He looked and smelled like he'd been on the trail a few days. "Did you have any trouble?"

"Not a bit. It took me a while longer to find two cowboys willin' to make the drive. Seems nobody wants to take a chance on crossin' Buck Lincoln. But Willow and Pad said they owed Lincoln a thing or two." Rand chuckled as he pushed his floppy hat back. "They once worked for him and he fired 'em without pay. It seems Lincoln took Brindle's word over theirs about some horses they'd been breakin'. Brindle out and out lied, but Willow said they couldn't prove it."

"Brindle and his men are at the house right now."

"You don't say!"

Maple giggled and told the story.

Rand slapped his thigh and laughed. "We got us some fun in store. Wait'll Willow and Pad hear about this."

Just then a cow and her calf broke away from the herd. Maple urged her horse forward and easily hazed the cow and calf back with the others. She had helped herd cattle from the time she could stay on a cow pony that had been trained to turn mid-air if need be.

About an hour later the cattle were milling around inside the pasture or drinking at the big wooden tank. The shorthorn stood by itself in the shade of a cottonwood. Maple had noticed it wasn't branded. She smiled in satisfaction as she walked beside Rand and the cowboys toward the house. The cowboys were in their early twenties, both tall, and both tough. Willow was blond and Pad was a black man.

"Lucy will have supper ready," Maple said. She grinned at Rand. He'd asked her to keep Brindle and his men a secret from Willow and Pad. Rand had said that would be their bonus for doing a good job.

"Who is Lucy?" Rand asked as they neared the pump.

"She's a girl from St. Louis who needs a home for a while." Maple couldn't bring herself to tell Rand the whole story.

Just then Willow spotted Brindle tied up under

the tree. "Am I seein' things?" he asked, rubbing his eyes.

Pad stepped closer, then grinned. "'Peers like we got us a party."

They turned to Maple for the story.

She told them and ended with, "They'll be coming around before long. But we don't want trouble."

"Me and Pad just might take these boys for a long ride deep in the sandhills and leave 'em on foot," Willow said with a chuckle. "We can tie 'em on their horses, drop 'em off, and take their horses with us. What say, Pad, my boy?"

"I like it," Pad said.

Rand slapped them on their backs. "After you boys drop 'em off you'd best head for Wyoming or Colorado to find work there."

"Good idea," Willow said as he bent to pump water for Pad and Rand.

Just then Lucy stepped out the door, a dish towel in her hand, and the wind tugging at her skirt and hair. "Supper's ready, you all."

Rand whistled softly. "She's a real beauty, Maple. If she can cook as good as she looks, I might hang around a bit."

Maple frowned at Rand. She had never thought about him being interested in anything but his art and meadowlark nests. "She's a nice girl, Rand. Don't you break her heart."

"Me? Would I do that?"

Maple saw the twinkle in Rand's eye and shook her head.

A few minutes later Maple introduced Lucy to

Rand, Willow, and Pad.

"I'm delighted to meet you," Lucy said to all three of them, but her gaze stayed the longest on Rand. He never took his eyes off her except to fill his plate.

Over supper Rand kept Lucy talking. Willow and Pad ate quickly, then excused themselves to get Brindle and his men loaded up. Maple knew Rand had already paid them and they were free to go whenever they wanted. She convinced them to tie the men to their horses sitting up instead of belly-flopped over their saddles. The men came to, but not enough to know what was happening to them. Willow strung three of the horses together for him to lead and Pad did the same with the other three. They rode west saying they wouldn't stop until they were too tired to keep going.

"We might head right for the Pacific Ocean," Willow called back as he turned to wave to Maple.

Laughing, she waved back. Brindle and his men were gone, hopefully for good. She had a pasture of cattle that needed branding. She thought of Hadley and sighed.

From inside the house she heard Lucy and Rand laughing. Lucy seemed taken with Rand and Maple felt strangely responsible for her.

Later Rand milked the cow while Maple and Lucy did the dishes. The house felt too warm. Maple was thankful for the occasional breeze that blew in.

"I looked at the sod house again," Lucy said, flushing slightly. "And I have an idea."

Maple tensed. "Oh?"

Lucy wound the dishtowel around her hand. "Could we fix it for me? I could live there until I know where I'm going. I'd help around here, but be out of your way when you wanted privacy."

Maple bit her lip. Did she want Lucy out of the house at night, leaving her alone with Hadley? "I'll think about it."

Rand walked in with the milk and Maple took it to strain it.

"I made a yellow cake," Lucy said softly as she looked up at Rand. Her cheeks were flushed and her eyes sparkled. "Would you like a piece with a cup of coffee?"

"Sure would." Rand sat at the table and watched Lucy cut a piece of cake. His dark eyes were hooded. He looked at ease.

Maple rolled her eyes. Maybe *she* should move to the sod house and give Lucy and Rand privacy. She knew they didn't notice when she carried the milk out to cool in the well.

In the dusk of the evening she walked toward the pasture, the wind teasing her hair. She still wore her levis and blue plaid shirt. She glanced back toward the house and sighed. Was she jealous of the attention Rand was giving Lucy? She frowned. "I have no right to be," she whispered hoarsely.

Just then she caught a movement near the barn. She froze. She couldn't make out what it was. Maybe the dogs? "Pete? Repete?" They didn't answer. She realized they hadn't run to her when she'd walked toward the pasture.

Silently she prayed for protection. She glanced toward the house. Could she make a run for it before whoever was there caught her?

Shivers tingled down her spine as she started toward the house, keeping as far away from the barn as she could. She heard a sound and her blood froze. Could it be Buck Lincoln? Wouldn't he have shot her on the spot?

"Maple," Hadley called softly from the shadows of the barn.

"Hadley!" She ran toward him, her heart leaping. "You're home!"

He caught her and pulled her into the shadows. Pete and Repete stood quietly beside him. "What's goin' on here?" he whispered sharply. "Who's the stranger in the house and where did the cattle come from?"

Maple blew out her breath as she leaned against the barn. "I have a lot to tell you, Hadd."

She had used his nickname and it sent a thrill through him. With all his willpower he ignored the feelings she aroused in him and tackled the problem at hand. It had felt strange to return to his place to see a cowboy with Maple and Lucy and to find the pasture full of cattle. "Suppose you tell me quick like."

She heard the steel in his voice and frowned. "The cowboy once worked for Papa. Rand Rawlings is his name."

"Rand Rawlings, you say!"

She nodded with a puzzled look at his reaction. "He ran across strays on the open range and I offered to buy them. He hired a couple of cowboys to help him and they got here late this afternoon."

Hadley narrowed his eyes. "It seems like you left a few things out of your story. Just when did the cowboy tell you about the strays?"

"Several days ago."

"And why didn't you mention it to me?" Hadley's voice was like icicles.

Maple swallowed hard. "I didn't . . . have a chance."

"And how do you expect me to pay for them?"

"I already did."

He gripped her arm. "*You* did? Since when do you have a say in *my* operation?"

His words stung her. "Since you forced me to come here with you," she snapped. "It's too bad you didn't let me stay with my folks. Then you would be free for your little mail-order bride!"

"And you'd be free for your cowboy!"

"What are you talkin' about?"

"Your pa told me why your momma was so set against you marryin' a ranch man. He said you once loved a cowboy named Rand Rawlings. Is this the same one?"

"Yes," Maple whispered.

"So he was all set to do you a favor. He brought strays to you."

"It wasn't like that at all, Hadd! Rand needed some money. He was going to sell them to Buck Lincoln. I thought we needed cattle."

"And how do you know they're strays?"

"They're not branded. And Rand wouldn't rustle

cattle." Tears burned the backs of her eyes. She had thought he would be pleased.

"You know that about him, do you? You haven't seen him for nine years. How do you know what he's become?"

Maple knotted her fists as anger rushed through her. In the distance a coyote yapped. From the house Rand laughed. "He's an artist if you must know!"

"Does paintings that hang in saloons, no doubt."

"You're jealous, Hadley Clements! Admit it!"

Hadley's stomach balled tightly. He *was* jealous! "I guess I am," he said hoarsely.

"You have no reason to be." Maple's eyes widened. Was he jealous because of her and Rand or because of Lucy and Rand?

Hadley was quiet a long time as he looked off toward the house. "I'm sorry. Forgive me?"

Maple bit back a whimper. It was Lucy and Rand! "I guess so."

"Take me to meet this wonderful cowboy."

Maple nodded as they slowly walked toward the house. "Lucy would like to fix up the sod house and live there for a while."

Hadley stopped short. "Why is she still here? You were both supposed to leave with Ed Turner."

Maple stamped her foot. "I told you I am staying no matter what. Why won't you believe me?"

"But why would you put Lucy in such danger?"

"Is that what's bothering you? She *wanted* to stay!"

"Oh. She did?" Hadley smiled.

Maple wanted to slap the smile off his face. How

dare he be pleased that Lucy wanted to stay? With her head high Maple walked to the house and stepped inside. The soft glow of the lamp shone across the table where Lucy and Rand still sat.

"I wondered where you'd got to," Lucy said. Then she jumped up. "Hadd! You're back. Hadd, this is Rand Rawlings. Rand, this is Maple's husband, Hadley Clements."

Rand pushed back his chair and stood. He eyed Hadley up and down.

Hadley studied Rand, trying to see why Maple had loved him. Finally Hadley shook hands with Rand. "Where did you pick up those strays?"

Rand told him. "I spotted them earlier this year, but left 'em alone, then when I needed cash money, I figured I'd round 'em up and sell 'em. Maple here struck a good deal with me. She's got her daddy's business head on her shoulders." Rand smiled at Maple.

"Thanks," she said, smiling proudly.

"Did Maple tell you what happened today?" Lucy asked as she held a cup of coffee out to Hadley.

"Did something happen besides the cattle?" Hadley set the cup on the table and rested his hands lightly on his hips as he studied Maple.

Before Maple could say anything Lucy told the whole story about Brindle and the toadstools.

Hadley gripped the back of a chair as he listened. He couldn't believe Maple had been in such danger and had calmly handled it. What if the men had learned her plan and killed her on the spot? He saw the pleased look on Maple's face and his anger increased. With a low growl he rushed out the door, slamming the screen door behind him. He walked out into the prairie and stopped on a grassy knoll. He lifted his face to the sky and shouted, "Father God, what kind of wife do I have? How can I live with such a one?"

In the yard Maple heard his shout, but couldn't make out the words. Why was he so angry with her? She'd gotten rid of Brindle and his men, hadn't she?

With her head down and her heart heavy Maple slowly walked back into the house. "I'm going to bed," she said just above a whisper. "Rand, you can sleep in the barn. Do you need a blanket?"

"I have my bedroll." Rand lifted her face with his hand under her chin. "What's wrong, Maple?"

Tears welled up in her eyes and she couldn't speak without breaking down. He smelled of sweat and leather.

"He's afraid for you," Rand whispered. "That's why he's angry."

Maple pulled away. What did Rand know? "Lucy, are you coming to bed?"

"In a minute." Lucy touched Maple's arm. "I didn't mean to make trouble."

"He'd have found out sooner or later. It surprises him that I can take care of myself." Actually it surprised her too. Momma had led her to believe she couldn't.

The next morning Maple slipped out of bed without waking Lucy, dressed, and walked to the kitchen. She stopped short. Hadley was asleep on a pallet on the floor. She looked down at him in his sleep. He lay on his back with one arm over the quilt across him and the other arm flung onto the floor. She envied his long, dark lashes. A dark stubble covered his lower face. She smiled as she thought about shaving him. He'd probably never let her touch him again.

Just then he opened his eyes. They were dark with an emotion she couldn't read. Slowly he sat up. He pulled on his shirt. She sank to the rocker, her legs suddenly shaky.

"Good morning," he said softly.

"Good morning," she whispered.

"I'm sorry I got so angry last night. I came back to tell you, but you'd already gone to bed." With the quilt as cover, he slipped on his levis. He knelt beside the rocker and looked deep into her eyes. "Will you forgive me?"

She barely nodded.

"We'll fix up the sod house for Lucy. Rand said he'd stay to help brand the cattle."

"You don't mind him being here?"

Hadley shook his head and smiled. "You're my wife. I trust you."

She didn't know if she trusted him with Lucy. But she couldn't say anything.

"You'd better change into your levis. We'll need you to help with branding."

Maple jumped up with a glad laugh. "I'll make breakfast, then change. Are you hungry?"

"As a bear!" He hadn't felt much like eating yesterday.

"I'll fix hash browns, eggs, bacon. Coffee. Biscuits 'n gravy."

Hadley laughed. He ran a finger down her hair and caught a braid in his hand. "I like red hair."

"Strawberry blonde."

"I hope our kids have your hair." He kissed her braid and let it fall to her shoulder.

She felt as if she had been kissed the way he kissed her before. The world seemed to stand still.

Hadley devoured her with his eyes. He started to reach for her. The bedroom door opened and Lucy walked in. Hadley turned to greet her with a forced smile. He would get the sod house in order yet today.

Maple took a deep, steadying breath, then walked to the stove to start the fire.

CHAPTER 8

Dressed in boots and levis, Maple stood beside the pasture fence with Hadley on one side of her and Rand on the other. Her wide-brimmed hat shielded the morning sun from her face. Dust billowed out from the milling cattle. Two calves ran and kicked up their heels. A horse whinnied in the corral beside the barn.

Hadley suddenly whistled in surprise and pointed. "That shorthorn bull belongs to Buck Lincoln!"

"How can that be?" Maple asked.

Rand slapped his leg. "I'll be hornswoggled! That's range justice for you."

Hadley narrowed his eyes. The shorthorn pawed the ground and snorted. "It turned up missin' a short time after he bought it. He sent his boys lookin' everywhere, but they couldn't find it. He figured it was long gone or dead."

Rand chuckled and scratched his head. "It was right in with the strays out on the open range north of his place. Probably wintered with 'em last winter." Rand clamped his hand on Hadley's shoulder. "It's not branded. I say let's brand him first."

"Let's do!" Maple cried, ready to go.

Hadley shook his head. "We can't. He belongs to Lincoln. We'll take him back."

"You been in the loco weed, Hadd?" Rand asked sharply.

"I don't see why we need to take him back after all Lincoln did to us," Maple said with a frown.

Hadley looked from Maple to Rand and back again. "That's how I work. It would be stealin' to keep the bull. I don't steal. We take the bull back first chance we have."

"I bought and paid for him!" Maple cried, her cheeks flushed bright red. "It's my say what we do with him!"

Hadley caught her hand and held it even when she tried to jerk free. "Maple, we do what God wants. He doesn't want us to steal. The other cattle are strays and we don't know if any of them belong to the ranchers around here. But the shorthorn is different. We do know. We have to do what's right."

Maple finally nodded. She did want to do what God wanted her to do. "I'll go with you tomorrow, Hadd."

"We'll see," Hadley said, turning away. He didn't want her near Lincoln when he told him about Brindle and his men. Lincoln had plenty of cowboys working for him, but Brindle had been hired to guard against homesteaders squatting on his land.

"I'll get the horses saddled," Rand said, heading for the barn.

Maple fell into step beside Hadley. "Lucy said she'd keep the fire going while we brand."

"She's real spunky for a city girl." Hadley nodded. "Real spunky."

Maple pressed her lips tightly together and walked faster.

"She's prettier than an apple tree in bloom," Rand said over his shoulder.

"Just get the horses saddled," Maple snapped.

A few minutes later Maple rode Twister into the pasture. Rand and Hadley were on foot. Lucy had the fire just right to heat the irons. Maple sent Twister after a young bull calf to cut it from the herd. Twister cut the calf away from the others and it raced across the pasture. Twister thundered after the calf. Maple swung her rope and sent it snaking over the head of the young calf. It settled easily around the calf's neck. She rode toward the branding area where Hadley and Rand waited beside the fire and the hot branding irons. Lucy had climbed over the fence to watch from the other side.

Twister stopped and stepped back, tightening the rope on the calf while Rand flipped it on its left side. Rand dropped to the ground in back of the calf, grabbed the calf's right hind leg and pulled it straight while he pushed its left hind leg forward with his booted foot. Hadley held the Rocking R brand to the calf's flank and pressed it down firmly. The smell of burning hair rose in the air. The calf bellowed and Lucy cried out. Rand set the calf free and it ran off to join the herd. Lucy left shortly after that. She said it was too much for her.

Maple coiled her rope as she turned Twister toward the herd to cut out another calf. Dust covered her and she was glad for the neckerchief over her mouth and nose. Time after time she roped a calf or cow. The bigger ones were harder for Rand to hold, but with all of them working together they finished the job before the middle of the afternoon. They didn't brand the shorthorn bull that belonged to Buck Lincoln even though she tried again to get Hadley to do it.

Tiredly they walked to the pump to wash. Maple's skin burned with sweat, heat, and dust. The icy water felt refreshing on her face, neck, and hands.

"You're crazy to take the shorthorn to Lincoln," Rand said as he washed off.

Hadley shrugged. Right was right and he wasn't going to argue about it. Crazy or not, it was the right thing to do no matter what Buck Lincoln had done to him.

"When are you going?" Maple asked as she dried her face and hands on a rough towel.

"Right after we eat."

Maple glanced toward the house where Lucy was making dinner. Smoke drifted up from the chimney and mixed with the blue of the bright summer sky. Pete and Repete lay near the door where Hadley had ordered them to stay during the branding. Without looking at him, Maple said, "I'm goin' with you, Hadd."

He frowned at her, then rolled his eyes. "You're too tough to argue with."

She grinned and wrinkled her nose at him. "It's about time you figured that out."

Lucy was quiet as she dished up the food and set it on the table.

"Country life too rough for you?" Rand asked, tugging a strand of Lucy's golden brown hair.

"I didn't know that's how the cattle got branded," she said as she sat beside Maple and across from Rand.

Rand smiled at Lucy. "Any gal that can travel all alone from St. Louis to these sandhills is tough enough to handle brandin'. Ain't that right, Hadd?"

"I reckon so." Hadley smiled at Lucy.

"Maybe I'm not cut out for ranch life after all." Lucy folded her hands in her lap and looked sad. "I might be better off married to a city man. A banker, maybe."

Maple frowned. What was Lucy up to? Was she serious or was she playing with Rand?

Hadley ended the discussion by praying over the food. He didn't know what Lucy was doing, but he didn't want to figure it out.

Maple filled her plate and talked about how much hay they'd need to winter the strays. She noticed Rand ate in silence, but darted a look at Lucy from time to time.

After dinner Hadley roped the shorthorn and led it out of the pasture. Rand closed the gate, a thoughtful look on his face. Maple looped her rope around the shorthorn's neck. She rode on one side and Hadley the other with the shorthorn in the middle. It was forced to walk along quietly without fighting the ropes.

"I'll clean the sod house while you're gone," Lucy shouted after them.

"I'll help her," Rand called, then laughed.

Maple looked back at them and rolled her eyes. Ed Turner didn't stand a chance with Lucy if Rand turned on all his charm.

As she rode away from the ranch Maple pulled her hat low enough to shield her face from the sun. She wanted to talk to Hadley, but she would have to shout to be heard, so she kept quiet. She looked at him and thought he was dozing in the saddle. She had learned to sleep in the saddle too, but she felt too tied in knots to consider sleeping. She wished she could crawl inside his brain to see what he was thinking.

The shorthorn bellowed and tried to stop, but the two ropes around his neck kept him walking. Both Twister and Champion were trained to keep the ropes taut.

In less than an hour they reached Buck Lincoln's ranch. The white frame two-story house was about four times as big as Hadley's. Gray shingles covered the roof and gray shutters hung at each window. A white picket fence with red, white, and yellow flowers swaying brightly in the wind circled the huge yard. Five cottonwoods shaded the house. Three barns, several sheds, a chicken house, bunk house and cookhouse dotted the prairie. A windmill whirled in the hot wind.

Hadley stopped near the small white gate that led into the yard. "Stand, Champion," he ordered as he slipped to the ground. He turned to Maple. "Do you want to wait here or come in with me?"

She thought of Buck Lincoln shooting Fuzzy and she trembled. Twister sidestepped to keep the rope tight. "I'll wait."

Hadley smiled. "I won't be long."

Before he could move, the door flew open and Buck Lincoln strode onto his porch and down the steps. A white hat covered his head. His right hand rested on the butt of his Colt. "Am I seein' things or is that my shorthorn you got there?" he growled in his gravelly voice.

"It's your bull," Hadley said, opening the gate for Lincoln. "Someone found it out on open range and brought it to me. I recognized it as yours and brought it back."

"I told him to keep it," Maple snapped. "But he wouldn't."

Buck frowned at Maple, then ignored her as he studied the shorthorn. "Looks in good shape."

"He is."

Buck studied the shorthorn closer. "You probably want to be paid for bringin' it back."

"Nope."

Maple bit her lip to keep back her angry answer.

Buck rested his hands lightly on his hips and studied Hadley. "This sure won't keep me from gettin' my range land back from you."

"It's my land and you won't get it." Hadley mounted in one easy movement. "Shall we take the shorthorn to your corral?"

Buck nodded. "The boys are out hayin'."

Hadley and Maple walked the shorthorn to the corral. Buck opened the gate and they turned the bull inside, then coiled up their ropes and draped them over their saddle horns. The shorthorn ran awkwardly to the tank and drank.

"It's a good lookin' animal," Buck said gruffly.

"Sure is."

Maple watched a rooster fly up on a fence and crow with its head back.

"When did you see Brindle last?" Hadley asked innocently as he dropped to the ground to stand at the fence with Buck.

Maple hid a grin.

Buck sputtered as he leaned against the corral. "What's it to you?"

"He and his men paid my wife a call." Hadley looped his arm around a fence post and rested his boot on the bottom rail of the fence.

"Not by my orders!" Buck snapped.

Maple curled her gloved hands over the saddle horn.

"They wanted dinner, so she cooked one for 'em. One they won't forget in a long time."

Buck shot a look at Maple. "Did you poison 'em?"

She lifted her chin and her eyes flashed. "Yes!"

Buck jerked up, his steel gray eyes wide in shock.

"I fed them toadstools in the stew. They got sick, but they didn't die. We sent them off where they won't find their way back for a long time. Maybe never."

"What's this?"

Hadley stepped right up to Buck. "We are stayin'

on our place! Nothin' you do will change that. Short of killin' us. Is that what you plan to do?"

Buck looked at Hadley, then at the shorthorn. "Why didn't you just keep the shorthorn?"

"I don't steal from anyone, not even from a man who kills my wife's kitten."

Buck's face darkened.

"I was for us keepin' the shorthorn," Maple said angrily. "But Hadd wouldn't hear of it. He's better at doin' what God wants than I am."

"But she's learnin'," Hadley said, winking at Maple.

She squared her shoulders and smiled in spite of herself.

Buck pushed his hat to the back of his head. "I never run across a religious man like you before." He rubbed a hand over the butt of his Colt. "I reckon I'll call off the fight. You keep my range. I'll go deeper in the sandhills."

"This time get it in writin'," Hadley said. "There's comin' a time when more homesteaders will be headin' for the sandhills. You don't want to be fightin' 'em all your life."

Buck nodded. "I reckon you're right. Times are changin'. For the worse. Was a time I fed my cattle all over them hills and not a man stopped me. Next thing, there'll be law in these parts."

"Not too soon for me," Maple said.

"She loved that kitten of hers," Hadley said softly.

Buck slammed his fist into his palm. "You want blood from me? I never apologized before and I ain't about to start now. You two get off my place. And be quick about it."

Hadley swung into the saddle. He tipped his hat to Buck Lincoln and motioned for Maple to lead the way.

Leaning low over the saddle, Maple urged Twister into a gallop on the road leading away from the ranch. She heard Hadley on Champion behind her. Finally she slowed Twister to a walk and turned in the saddle to watch Hadley slow Champion.

"Are you over your mad?" Hadley asked with a grin.

She narrowed her eyes and spat, "No!"

He rode up beside her and caught Twister's reins. "Want to talk?"

"What good will it do? You already gave Lincoln his shorthorn and you didn't do a thing about Fluffy!"

"Maple, God says we shouldn't pay back. We're to do good to our enemies. Repay evil with good."

"I'm not that way!"

"Yes, you are. You're a child of God. His Spirit dwells in you. With his help you can love your enemies."

"What if I don't want to?"

"Then I'll teach you God's Word so you'll want to." Hadley reached out and caught Maple's hand in his as their mounts walked slowly side by side, almost touching.

Maple sighed heavily. She struggled against showing Hadley how her pulse leaped at his touch.

She wished they had their gloves off so their hands really touched.

"Jesus said to forgive, Maple. So—you must."

Maple hung her head. She knew what Hadley said was true. Elly had showed her the verses in the Bible and she'd read them for herself. But forgiveness didn't come easy to a Raines. She was still a Raines even though her last name was now Clements. She asked for God's help so she could forgive.

Silently Hadley prayed for Maple. He knew when to keep quiet. He squeezed her hand as they rode side by side in silence. Up above an eagle soared through the vast blue sky. Hadley smiled. He'd shot at one when he was a boy. Pa had taken his belt to him to remind him never to do it again. He hadn't.

Had Pa received his letter yet telling them about his marriage to Maple? Sometimes letters made it home in a matter of days and other times it took weeks.

"Maple, how would you like to meet my family?"

Her eyes widened. "I don't know. They might not like me."

"Sure they will!" Hadley laughed excitedly. The idea to take Maple to his home had suddenly popped into his head. He realized he desperately wanted his family to know her. "We could ask Rand to stay on at our place after we're finished hayin', then we could visit my family."

"What about Lucy? It wouldn't look right to leave her at our place alone with Rand."

"We're not her keepers."

"I know."

"Maybe you don't want Rand to take an interest in her."

Maple frowned. "That's not true!"

"Sorry. I'm far from perfect no matter how I seem." He chuckled. "I want you to meet Pa and Ma and the kids. They're grown up kids, but they'll always be 'the kids' to me."

Maple moved uneasily. "Do we have to decide right now?"

"Nope." He rode in silence a few minutes, then turned to her again. "Made up your mind yet?"

She jerked her hand away from him and laughed, then urged Twister to a run.

"You're not gettin' away from me!" Hadley shouted as he sent Champion leaping after Maple. Hadley leaned low. The wind tugged at his hat and billowed out his shirt. Suddenly he whistled shrilly. It was a whistle that meant for Twister to stop. He'd trained him that way.

Twister stopped short, catching Maple unaware. She flew out of the saddle and over Twister's head. She'd learned years ago to relax and take a fall in a tumble. She lay still in the tall grass, her hat smashed under her.

Hadley's heart jerked to a stop. What had he done? He leaped from the saddle before Champion stopped. "Maple! Oh, my precious, darling Maple!" Hadley dropped to his knees and gently lifted Maple.

"Ohhhh," she groaned.

"I'm so sorry! I didn't mean for you to get hurt."
Hadley pushed his face into her hair and moaned
from deep inside.

"Ohhhh," she groaned again, harder this time.
Inside she was laughing. Hadley was getting just
what he deserved for making Twister stop.

"Please, Jesus, don't let her be hurt bad. I'm
sorry for bein' so thoughtless."

A giggle burst out of Maple before she could stop
it.

Hadley heard it and pushed her away enough to
look into her face. He saw her smile and saw the
mischief in her eyes. "You think you're pretty cute,
don't you?"

"Sure do." Maple squirmed out of his grasp and
jumped up. "Oh, my precious, darling Maple!" she
mimicked with a giggle.

He lunged at her and caught her around the legs,
sending her sprawling in the grass again. Laughing,
he sprawled over her and held her down. "You're a
big tease, you red-headed woman."

"Strawberry blonde," she said with a giggle.

"I love strawberries!" Laughing, he nuzzled her
hair.

His lips touched her cheek and she grew very
still. She smelled the tang of his skin and felt the
weight of his body on her.

He felt her softness and the tickle of her hair
against his face. The laughter died in his throat. He
trailed kisses across her cheek to her lips, then
kissed her with a passion that reached to the depth
of his heart.

Weakly she pushed against his chest. She felt his racing heart and knew hers was thundering even more than his.

He lifted his head and looked deep into her eyes. "I love you," he whispered hoarsely.

She gasped. He couldn't mean it! It was only his mood for the moment. "Let me go," she said weakly.

"No," he whispered. Gently, tenderly he stroked her lips with his and she closed her eyes and gave herself up to his embrace. He kissed her eyelids and her high flat cheeks, then again her lips.

She moaned and returned his kiss.

Finally he sat up and pulled her up into his arms. They sat in the tall prairie grass with their horses beside them for a long, long time.

CHAPTER 9

Maple wiped sweat from her face as she urged the team forward to rake the cut hay into windrows. She sat high on the round seat. Her hands burned inside her gloves and the tug of the reins hurt her arms. Today was the last day of haying and she was glad. It was a hot, tiring job. Obid and Tad along with Rand had been helping them for the past week. Hay stacks dotted the range all around them. She watched Hadley and his team of horses take the sweep to another windrow, pick up hay on the long teeth, and carry it to the stacker that lifted it up on the mound of hay. Maple frowned as she saw Hadley wipe sweat from his face. He'd withdrawn the past few days and acted as if he had never held her and kissed her as she imagined a husband kissed his wife. But maybe it was because of Lucy always being there. She and Rand had fixed the sod house, but Rand was staying in it until after haying when he could get his wagon back.

Just before dark Maple wearily turned her team into the corral as Obid and Tad rode for home. The haying crew had worked until the job was done and she knew they were as tired as she was. Her stomach growled with hunger. When Lucy had fed them at noon Hadley told her to wait supper until they finished. Slowly Maple pulled off her gloves and hat. She tugged her braid free and ruffled her hair as she watched Hadley and Rand put the rake and sweep beside the shed. Warm wind dried the sweat on her head and face. How she longed for a bath!

At the pump she washed with icy water that made her skin tingle. Sitting on the bench, she wearily pulled off her boots and socks. Inside her levis her legs burned.

Looking hot and tired in her calico dress and flowered apron, Lucy walked from the house and sat beside Maple. "I did the chores and got supper ready."

"Thanks. I'm starving, but I feel too tired to eat."

"Maple, why would you ever want this life instead of life with Ed Turner where you would be waited on?"

Maple frowned. "I'm tired, but I like to work. I like to see what I've accomplished at the end of the day."

"But you turn right around and do the same thing the next day! Your work never gets done."

"I know."

"And when you have kids, it'll be even worse."

Maple studied Lucy thoughtfully. "Are you thinkin' about yourself?"

Lucy flushed and turned away slightly.

"Are you afraid if you married Rand your life would be harder than if you married Ed Turner?"

Maple leaned close to Lucy. "What about love? You said you wouldn't marry unless you loved and were loved."

Her eyes glistening with tears, Lucy turned to Maple. "I could love them both. It's just that Rand is so exciting to listen to and talk to. Ed is . . ."

"A stuffed shirt."

Lucy giggled and nodded. "But I do care about him! I really do."

"Has Rand told you he doesn't do much cowboyin' any more?"

Lucy frowned. "No. What do you mean?"

"Ask Rand. You might be surprised." Maple watched Rand and Hadley coming toward them. They both walked as if they were used to the saddle more than being on foot. Hadley was taller and leaner and a few years younger than Rand. They both were covered with dust and particles of hay and looked bone weary.

"Supper's ready," Lucy called to them.

"Bring it to me where I fall and pour it down my gullet," Rand said with a low chuckle.

Hadley tossed his hat to land at Maple's feet, then he pumped water and splashed it over his face and head. He dried off and slicked his hair back with his comb. "I'm takin' off my boots. You girls might want to get downwind from me." He plopped to the ground beside them and struggled with his boot.

Maple jumped up catching one boot and pulling it off, then the other. She smiled at him and he smiled back. "I draw the line at socks," she said with a self-conscious laugh as she dropped back on the bench. What had possessed her to pull off his boots? Would he think she was asking for more of his kisses?

Hadley wanted to pull Maple into his arms and hold her close, but he turned to Rand instead. "I reckon you'll be headin' out now that the hayin' is done."

Rand glanced at Lucy, then shrugged.

"If you're in no hurry, I could use you to do chores for me while Maple and I go visit my family. There's not much pay, but free room and board."

Rand scratched his head. "Can I let you know?"

"Sure. But we want to leave in a couple of days."

Maple locked her hands together. It was going to be hard to meet Hadley's family.

Lucy jumped up, her face red. "I'm in the way again! I'm always in the way!" She burst into tears and ran to the house, her skirts swishing around her ankles.

"What's wrong with her?" Hadley asked.

"I'll see." Rand strode to the house and closed the screen door quietly after him.

Hadley straddled the bench beside Maple and slipped his arms around her. He saw her cheeks turn pink and felt her stiffen. "We'll sleep out under the stars and have a real honeymoon. Will you like that?"

Shivers ran up and down her spine. "Are you teasing me again?"

He nuzzled her ear. "We'll lay out on the prairie under the stars, just you 'n me. We'll pluck a star from the sky for our cover."

"Please don't. You're embarrassing me."

He kissed her cheek, then jumped up. "Let's go eat supper. I know you're as hungry as I am." He pulled her up and caught her close in a brief hug. He picked up their boots and walked to the house with her, whistling *Home On the Range*.

She turned hot, then cold, and wondered if she could even eat with him so close.

Inside the house the lamp shone in the middle of the table. It was set for four as usual. Heat poured from the stove, making the kitchen almost unbearable. The bedroom door was open and Lucy was sobbing while Rand tried to comfort her.

"Come eat and you'll feel better," Hadley called as he dropped the boots with a thud beside the door. He grinned at Maple and whispered, "A lover's quarrel."

Maple frowned, then dished up the fried chicken, boiled potatoes, gravy, and buttered corn. She cut the cornbread and set it on the table beside the thick mound of fresh butter.

"Lucy, Rand! Get in here and eat," Hadley called. "You can hash all your troubles over later."

Brushing tears away, Lucy walked from the bedroom with Rand behind her.

"She thinks she should go back to her aunt," Rand said gruffly.

Maple caught Lucy's hand. "No! Don't you dare do it, Lucy! You're free of her and you're going to stay free!"

Lucy smiled weakly. "Are you sure?"

Maple nodded. "You're just hungry and tired and

afraid because we're going away."

Finally they sat at the table, Hadley prayed and they ate in silence. Maple could still feel the sway of the rake and the tug of the reins on her arms.

Rand drank half his water and set the glass down. "If it's all the same to you, Hadd, I'd like to get my wagon and bring it here before you leave."

"Sure. Where is it?"

"In Keene. Behind the school house. Nick Birta is watching it for me."

"Why don't you let Lucy ride along with you?" Maple asked. "It'd give her a chance to get to town again. Maybe see a friend." She meant Ed Turner and she could tell Lucy knew it.

Lucy shook her head, her face pale. "I can't, Maple." She threw down her napkin. "Oh, it's all too confusing!"

"God imparts wisdom to anyone who asks," Hadley said gently.

Lucy nodded. "I guess I forgot to ask," she whispered.

"We'll pray together after supper when we have our devotions," Maple said. Almost every night except the past three when they were too tired to hold up their heads, Hadley had read a few verses from the Bible and they all prayed together. At first she was uncomfortable, but then she had grown to appreciate it as much as Lucy and even Rand.

After the dishes were finished they all gathered around the lamp at the table again. A moth flew against the screen door. Pete snapped at it, then

Repete did. An owl hooted from the barn.

Hadley opened his Bible and read First Corinthians, the second chapter. When he finished he led in a short prayer, making sure he prayed for Lucy.

The next morning Maple opened her eyes, then sat bolt upright. The sun was already high in the sky. She jumped out of bed, then laughed. The haying was finished and it wasn't urgent for her to be up and about. She peeked out the window, then frowned. Hadley and Lucy stood near the sod house deep in conversation. Jealousy ripped through Maple and took her breath away.

"How cozy. How very cozy," she whispered angrily.

Quickly she dressed in her green dimity, brushed her hair down on her shoulders, and clipped it back with two combs. Was Lucy reluctant to go with Rand because she didn't want to be away from Hadley?

Maple doubled her fists and pressed her lips tightly together. She walked to the door, her shoes loud against the plank floor. Just as she pushed open the screen door Pete and Repete barked to say someone was coming. "Who on earth is it?" Maple snapped, letting the screen door slam behind her. Chickens scratched in the yard. A calf bawled. Lucy and Hadley looked off in the direction the dogs were barking.

Maple took a deep breath. Was she going to let jealousy ruin her day? "Help me, Father God," she whispered. "I don't want to be jealous." She frowned. Why was she jealous anyway? She avoided the question and the answer as if it was a hot branding iron.

With her head high she walked across the yard and stopped beside Lucy and Hadley. "Good morning," she said, keeping her voice light. "Who's coming?" She shielded her eyes with her hand. Huge cottony clouds dotted the wide blue sky. A big black crow cawed and flew up from the ground.

"I don't know." Hadley stepped to her side. "Maybe Obid Smith."

Maple tensed. "Could it be Buck Lincoln?"

"I doubt it."

"I never want to see him!" Lucy cried.

Hadley smiled at Maple. "Did you sleep well?"

Maple nodded. "But you should have called me."

"No reason to. Lucy fixed breakfast while I did the chores."

Maple's stomach knotted, but she managed to keep a smile on her face. "Did Rand get off all right?"

"He left at dawn without even saying goodbye." Lucy bit her lip. "That wasn't very nice of him. I sure hope he comes back."

"He will," Hadley said.

Just then the rider rounded a hill and came into full view. He was on a roan and riding flat out. A dust cloud billowed out behind him.

"I'll be." Hadley stepped forward with a worried frown. "It's Brenner. Buck Lincoln's foreman. Somethin's up."

Maple moved closer to Hadley.

"Is he dangerous?" Lucy whispered.

Pete and Repete leaped forward, barking loudly. Hadley called them to heel and they slowly walked to him and sank at his feet.

Brenner pulled in the roan and dismounted before the gelding stopped. He was in his mid-forties with broad shoulders and lean hips. He jerked off his Stetson hat and faced Hadley squarely. "Buck's been hurt bad. I know you got no call to help him. But I'm hopin' you will. Obid said your woman knows doctorin'."

Maple sucked in her breath.

Hadley nodded. "How can she help?"

"No!" Lucy cried. "You can't ask her to!"

Hadley ignored Lucy and turned to Maple. "It's only right."

Maple closed her eyes and groaned. She looked at Brenner. "What happened to him?"

Brenner lifted a questioning brow to Hadley.

"Answer her."

Brenner nervously rolled his hat brim as he faced Maple. "Got snagged on that dad-burned barbed wire and got his leg cut real deep before we could stop his horse and get him free."

"I'll be ready in a minute."

"I'll go too," Hadley said as he ran toward the barn to saddle the horses.

In the house Maple pulled off her dress and underskirts and slipped on her levis and cotton shirt, tied her hair back in a long tail, and tugged on her boots.

"What can I do?" Lucy asked from the doorway.

"Get my bag."

"I already did. It's on the table." Lucy caught

Maple's arm. "I've been riding a lot. I won't be a bother. I promise. I just can't stay here alone!"

"Come on then. You'll be able to help me with Lincoln." Maple grabbed up her bag and her hat and ran outdoors where Hadley had three horses ready. He'd already guessed Lucy would want to go.

Hadley tied Maple's bag to the back of Twister's saddle. "You go on ahead with Brenner. Lucy and I will be right behind you."

Maple nodded, then swung into the saddle. She saw Brenner had borrowed a fresh horse. She urged Twister up beside Brenner and he spurred his horse into a run. She leaned low in the saddle and raced beside Brenner on the way to help their enemy, Buck Lincoln. Wind burned her face and chapped her lips. Her mind whirled with what might be ahead for her.

At the ranch a cowboy took Twister to the corral while Brenner led her to the house at a run and on into a bedroom on the main floor. The room was full of dark, highly polished furniture. An oval braided rug lay at the side of the wide bed. The high headboard and shorter footboard were intricately carved with flowers and leaves. Moaning and tossing, Buck Lincoln lay on the bed, his right leg covered with blood, his levis ripped. Maple bit her lip. Rusty barbed wire cuts infected fast.

Maple dropped her hat on the chest at the foot of the bed and rolled up her sleeves. "I need plenty of hot water."

"I told Sammy to have it ready. He's Buck's cook." Brenner hurried out, careful to keep his boots quiet on the floor.

Maple leaned over Buck just as he opened his eyes. "I came to help you."

"I never . . . asked you . . . to."

"Brenner came and got me. I know what I'm doing, so please try to lie quietly and let me tend you." Maple pulled scissors from her bag and snipped the pant leg off and dropped it in a heap on the floor. Bloody jagged tears ran down Buck's hairy leg from just above his knee down the side of his leg.

"It's bad. Ain't it?"

"Yes, but I can take care of it. I've worked on cowboys in worse shape than this." Impatiently she looked at the door. Where was the hot water? She had to clean the wounds immediately. She bent down to Buck. "I'll be right back. Please stay very still."

He moaned with his eyes closed tightly.

Maple ran to the door just as Brenner hurried in with a bucket of hot water and a wash basin. Maple frowned at him, but he shook his head slightly, so she didn't ask what had taken so long.

Quickly she cleaned Buck's leg. Just as she finished, Lucy and Hadley stopped in the doorway. "Take this, Lucy." Maple held out the basin and Lucy took it, her face pale.

"What can I do?" Hadley asked.

"Help Brenner hold him down while I sew his leg the best I can." Maple readied the needle and thread. She hated barbed wire tears! The clean cut of a knife was much easier to work on. With a silent prayer she started to work. Buck groaned, but never cried out even though she knew the pain was great. She caked his leg with a thick poultice and wrapped it with clean bandages. "Lucy, go to the kitchen and bring some soup for him."

Brenner pulled Maple aside. "The cook ran off and there's nobody in the kitchen."

"Show Lucy the kitchen and she'll take care of everything." Maple patted Lucy's arm. "Won't you?"

She nodded weakly, then followed Brenner out.

"Hadd Clements," Buck said gruffly.

Hadley bent over him. "I'm here."

"Why are you doin' this?"

"You needed help."

Buck's eyes filled with tears and he quickly turned his head away. "Get out of here! Give a man some rest!"

Hadley turned to Maple. "What else can I do?"

"Help me undress him and make him comfortable."

"No woman's gonna undress me!"

Maple sighed heavily. "Then Hadd will help you and call me in when you're properly covered." She walked out of the bedroom and stood in the wide hallway. Pictures of horses and cowboys lined the walls. She could hear Lucy and Brenner in the kitchen. The rest of the rooms were as silent as a deserted house.

"Maple," Hadley called.

She hurried back in. Buck's face was wet with sweat. She soaked a clean cloth and wiped away the sweat, then blotted his face dry. She lifted his head slightly and told him to drink some water. She could tell from his breath that he had whiskey before she came.

"I . . . shot your cat," Buck whispered hoarsely.

"I forgave you for it." She eased his head back on the pillow. "Rest and when the soup's ready, I'll feed you."

"Why'd you . . . forgive me?"

"Jesus said to." Maple brushed back Buck's gray hair. She had actually forgiven the man who brought them grief! She was going to stay and take care of him! Indeed she was learning to be more like Jesus just like Hadley had prayed for her!

Buck turned to Hadley. "Go to the barn and get a . . . cat for . . . her."

"That's not necessary," Maple said.

"Get it, Hadd!"

"I'll get it before we leave." Hadley smiled. "You rest a spell. We'll look out for you."

Maple opened the windows and let the breeze blow in. She was thankful the wind wasn't blowing in the barnyard smells. Tomorrow she'd get Buck outdoors and expose his wounds to the healing power of the sun. She stood at the window and looked out at the vast empire that belonged to Buck Lincoln. He was of the old breed just like Papa. Buck belonged deeper in the sandhills where all the range was still open and no homesteader had the nerve to travel.

Lucy brought in a bowl of soup while Brenner stopped in the doorway. "I'll feed him, Maple," she said softly. "I know you're tired."

"Thank you." Maple sank to a chair and leaned her head back. What had made Lucy change her mind and decide to help Buck Lincoln?

Hadley propped Buck up with several pillows as he said, "This is Lucy Everett, Buck. She's a guest at our place for a while and a mighty good cook."

Buck looked at her closely. "You won't poison me, will you?"

Lucy chuckled. "I could've, but I didn't. Open wide." She held out a spoon of beef broth and Buck swallowed it. She told him about St. Louis while she fed him the entire bowl. "Tomorrow I'll see that you get steak."

"I already got a cook."

Brenner stepped forward. "Sammy took off, Buck. He won't be back."

"Will the whole place fall apart because I'm under the weather?"

"I'll see to the ranch. I don't know about here in the house."

"I could stay and help," Lucy said. She shot a look at Hadley and Maple. "If that's all right."

Hadley shrugged.

"What'll we tell Rand?" Maple asked.

Lucy flipped her head. "I don't care! If he cares enough to ask about me, tell him I'm here."

"You got a job as housekeeper and cook if you want it," Buck said gruffly. "Is twenty a month and a room of your own enough?"

Maple could tell Lucy was going to agree. "She'll think about it," Maple said before Lucy could speak.

"I'll think on it," Lucy said.

"Your own buggy and one day a week to drive to town."

"She'll think about it," Hadley said, guiding Lucy and Maple out the door. "You rest, Buck. We'll check in on you later."

"Brenner, show Hadd my new stallion." Buck lifted his head. "Get me up and let me show you!"

Maple ran to the bed and pushed Buck down. "You will not leave this bed today! Stay quiet and get some sleep!"

"Yes, ma'am." Buck smiled, then frowned and closed his eyes.

Maple walked out of the room. "He'll need someone to make sure he stays put."

"I'll stay," Lucy said.

Maple looked at her in surprise. What had made Lucy change her mind about Buck Lincoln? Maple glanced at Hadley. Had he talked to her about what Jesus wanted?

Buck lifted his head again. "Get her a cat or I'll have your hide!"

Maple chuckled as she followed Hadley and Brenner to the front door. Suddenly her legs trembled and she felt light-headed. "I'll rest a bit and look at the stallion later."

"You all right, Maple?" Hadley asked in concern. He saw the pallor of her face.

"I just need to sit down."

"Go right on in the front room," Brenner said.

"I'll be back in later. With a kitten." Hadley smiled at her and followed Brenner out.

In the front room Maple sat in a wide blue chair and propped her feet up on the matching footstool. With a ragged sigh she closed her eyes. A picture of her wedding day flashed across her mind. Oh, how she had longed to ride off across the prairie far away from Ed Turner! If she was in that same situation today, would she stay?

"I'd run," she whispered with a tiny giggle. It felt good to know she had changed, had become strong enough to do what was right.

She thought about the trip ahead of her with Hadley. Did she have the courage to become his true wife? She flushed and shook her head. "I'm not as brave as I thought," she whispered hoarsely.

CHAPTER 10

Astride Twister and almost home again, Maple stroked the black and white kitten Buck Lincoln had given her two days ago. It had four white legs and a white tail. "Breeches, I never thought I'd see the day Buck Lincoln would become a friend."

Hadley looked back over his shoulder. "You talkin' to me?"

"To Breeches." Maple urged Twister forward to walk beside Hadley on Champion. "I'm glad Buck changed his mind about us."

"Me, too." Hadley leaned toward Maple. "Now, if you'd change your mind about me, we'd all be happy."

She flushed. "I don't know what you mean?"

"Oh, yes you do!" Hadley chuckled. "One of these days you'll look at me and say, 'That guy's not so bad. I love him.' Then you'll find the courage to tell me to my face. And with Lucy gone, you might find the courage sooner instead of later."

Maple skittered away from that subject like Pete and Repete did from a rattlesnake. "I'm glad Lucy decided to stay on with Buck. She said she would have time to see what's in her heart now that she has a home and a job."

"I'd say Rand's in her heart."

"I thought so too. He didn't tell her he was an artist instead of a cowboy. I wonder why."

"Could be he thinks she believes bein' a cowboy is more romantic than bein' an artist." Hadley chuckled. "You know how you womenfolk like romance."

Maple scowled at him. "Did I ever say that?"

"Nope. But you're a woman, Maple Clements, and that means you like romance as well as the next one." Just then they rounded a hill and could see the Rocking H. "We got company again." Hadley wanted to take Maple and ride away where they could be together alone, but he urged Champion into a run. Some of Buck's valuable horses that he'd agreed to train were in his corral. He couldn't have someone drop by and steal them.

Maple breathed a sigh of relief. She still wasn't ready to be alone with Hadley. She urged Twister to a trot and stopped him at the corral where Hadley stood with several people.

His face alight with excitement, Hadley ran to her side. "It's my family, Maple! They got here a few minutes ago."

Maple wanted to run away, but she slipped off Twister and walked beside Hadley to a crowd of people. She kept Breeches close against her.

"This is my wife, Maple," Hadley said proudly with his arm around her waist. "Pa—Morgan Clements. Ma—Laurel Clements." Hadley pointed as he called each name. "Diana, Alane, Maureen. These big cowboys are Worth, Garrett, and Forster."

They all talked at once as they tried to hug her. Her heart dropped to her feet. Were they crazy? Why should they hug her? They didn't even know her. And she sure didn't know them!

"Let's give her breathin' space," Morgan Clements said with a grin. He was in his early fifties with gray hair at his temples and dark eyes with deep laugh lines at the corners. He was a little shorter and heavier than Hadley and very good looking.

"What a pretty kitten," Maureen said as she stroked it. She was sixteen and had brown braids hanging down from her calico bonnet. Her eyes were as brown as Hadley's. "May I hold it?"

Reluctantly Maple handed Breeches to Maureen. "His name is Breeches and he's new to the place. He hasn't made friends with Pete and Repete yet."

"We'll show him around," Alane said as she looked toward the sod house where Rand stood. She was eighteen, petite, and very pretty with brown hair and eyes.

Diana touched Maple's arm. Diana's blue eyes were clouded with dark rings around them. She swayed slightly. "May I go inside out of the heat and sit down?"

"Of course!" Maple just then realized Diana was expecting a baby.

Looking concerned, Worth stepped to Diana's side. He had her same blond hair and blue eyes. He was almost as tall as Hadley and just as lean. "Should I carry you?"

Diana laughed and shook her head. "I'm not crippled, little brother, just tired."

"May I come in with you two?" Laurel asked, smiling warmly at Maple. She was shorter than Maple, slender, with graying brown hair and brown eyes. "The men want to look at the horses and the girls at your cowboy." Laurel chuckled. "I'll be glad when they're both married so I don't have to be concerned about every cowboy they meet. But they're good girls even though they do flirt a little. I really don't have to worry about them."

"You really don't, Ma," Diana said with a smile as they slowly walked toward the house.

"Rand's a Christian," Maple said. "He's not a womanizer like a lot of the cowboys are. But he does know how to turn on the charm."

"The girls know how to handle that," Diana said. She swayed and caught Maple's arm. "Sorry. But the wagon trip was harder than I thought it would be. I couldn't miss out on meeting you, though."

Inside the house Maple helped Diana to the rocking chair, then gave her a glass of cold water from the water bucket. She was glad Rand had filled it fresh from the well.

"This is a very cozy kitchen," Laurel said as she gazed around. "You've fixed it very pretty, Maple."

"Thank you." Her words warmed Maple and made her relax a little. "The bedroom's through that door. Some day we'll probably build on."

"You'll want to once you have babies," Diana

said.

Maple forced back a blush. She didn't want to talk about babies or the future. "Please sit down, Mrs. Clements, while I make dinner."

"I'd rather help, if you don't mind. It's very hard for me to sit by while someone else is working." Laurel untied her bonnet and hung it on a peg near the door. She rolled up the sleeves of her calico dress and asked for an apron. "You tell me what to do and I'll do it."

"I'll make stew."

"Then let me cut up the vegetables and start them cooking."

Soon Maple was working with Laurel as easily as she had with Lucy. When Diana felt better she stirred up a batch of biscuits and put them in to bake.

Maple told them about the trouble with Buck Lincoln and how it had been resolved. She even told them about Lucy Everett coming to marry Hadley only to find he was already married.

Diana told Maple about her husband, Seth, and their ranch, then Laurel told about theirs.

"Hadd and I were going to come visit you," Maple said with a laugh. "And here you come instead."

"We decided to come as soon as haying was done," Laurel said. "So we did."

"We would have met halfway if Buck Lincoln hadn't needed my help."

"It would have been funny if we ended up here and you at Pa's," Diana said, giggling.

Maple thickened the gravy in the stew. The tantalizing aroma teased her nostrils and the heat burned her face. "I sure don't know how I'll sleep all of you in this small house." She shrugged, then turned back to stir the stew. "Any suggestions?"

Laurel nodded. "The women can take the house and the men the barn, the sod house, or under the stars."

"Sounds good to me." Diana sank back in the rocking chair. Her red calico fell over her rounded stomach and hung down her slender legs to the tops of her hightop shoes. "Sleeping under the stars last night wasn't as bad as I thought, but I'd rather not do it again tonight."

Maple rested the wooden spoon across the stew pot, then turned to face Laurel and Diana. "You two can have the bed. The girls and I will sleep in here on pallets."

"I should argue about that, but I won't," Laurel said with a laugh.

A few minutes later Maple called everyone in to eat. They agreed to fix their food and eat outdoors on the ground. The house was too hot from cooking dinner.

Hadley held the screen door open for everyone to walk in. The kitchen seemed very small with so many in it. He slipped his arm around Maple and said, "Pa, will you ask the blessin' on the food?"

"Sure will." Morgan bowed his head with his arm around Laurel. "Heavenly Father, thank you for the wonderful new daughter you gave us. Bless Hadd and Maple and may they continue to grow in you. Thank you for this food. Bless the ones who

prepared it. In Jesus' Name. Amen." He smiled
around the kitchen. "This family is sure blessed!"
He pulled Laurel close and kissed her.

Maple's cheeks burned with embarrassment. In
all her twenty-five years she had never seen Papa
kiss Momma. Hadley's folks didn't seem to mind a
bit.

Hadley carried the rocker out for Diana while his
brothers carried the chairs and table out. The girls
sat on the ground on either side of Rand and kept him
talking and laughing. Morgan and Laurel sat at the
table with Maple and Hadley.

"You two have a nice place here," Morgan said,
nodding his head. "Hadd told me about the strays
you bought, Maple. Those strays make good
healthy stock. They can winter better than
Whitefaces or Herefords."

Maple puffed up with pride. It felt strange to
have Hadley's folks praise her. She couldn't remember a day going by that Momma hadn't scolded
her and berated her for her actions. But maybe she
was getting better. If they saw her now, they might
have only good things to say to her and about her.

"The boys said they'd help me train Buck's
horses," Hadley said as he spread butter on a split
biscuit.

"We're stayin' only a couple of days," Morgan
said. "Wish we could stay longer, but we can't
expect Seth to do our work as well as his for too
long. Seth is Diana's husband."

"I sure never expected her to marry him," Hadley
said in a low voice. "How do they get along?"

"Real well as far as we know," Morgan said.

"He didn't want Diana to come with us, but she did anyway," Laurel said. "Diana's a little headstrong for him."

Morgan leaned over and kissed Laurel. "You raised her that way."

"Better to be headstrong than a whipping post!"

"I agree," Maple said with a laugh.

"Don't give Maple any more ideas than she already has." Hadley reached over and tugged a strand of her hair. "She can be quite a handful when she puts her mind to it."

"Just the way you like her, right son?" Morgan chuckled.

Hadley nodded and winked at Maple.

She wanted to sink out of sight, but she managed to smile and continue eating.

On the third day when the family was leaving, Maple hated to see them go. She had learned to love all of them, especially Worth. He had a gentle heart and was aware of pain in others. She had overheard him giving Rand advice about Lucy. Rand had said goodbye earlier and was on his way to visit Lucy for the first time since she'd left.

Maple hugged each of the family, then watched as Hadley did the same.

"Come see us again," Maple said with a catch in her voice.

"And you come see us," Laurel said, kissing Maple's cheek.

The kiss touched Maple's heart deeply. Momma had never kissed her as long as she could remember.

Morgan hugged Maple again and kissed both cheeks. "Hadd's blessed to have you as his wife. You're a fine woman."

"Thank you," Maple whispered around the lump in her throat. She watched them climb into the buckboard. Morgan drove with Laurel and Diana beside him. The girls sat in the other seat and the boys on the back with their feet hanging over.

Tears filled Hadley's eyes. He circled Maple's waist with his arm for comfort and to give comfort. She was as teary-eyed as he was at their leaving. Whining, Pete and Repete sat at Hadley's feet. Breeches was asleep in his box in the house.

Maple slipped her arm around Hadley. Together they watched the buckboard until it was a dot on the endless prairie. "They're gone," Maple whispered.

Hadley nodded and swallowed hard to keep from sobbing. He turned to Maple, wrapping both his arms around her, and pressed his face into her mass of strawberry blonde hair. She clung to him, her cheek pressed against his chest, her eyes closed. She felt his heart thud against her and smelled the tang of his skin.

Finally he lifted his head. "I have to help Obid with a horse he's trainin'. Want to come?"

Maple nodded. "I'd hate to be alone now."

"I know." Hadley brushed his lips against hers. "I'm glad you like my family. They sure do love you."

"They do?"

Hadley nodded. "But not near as much as *I* love

you."

Her heart jerked strangely. He sounded like he meant it.

"What beautiful big blue eyes you have!" Hadley held her face between his hands and kissed her lips, her eyelids, and her lips again. "Tell me you love me. Please tell me."

Maple pushed against his chest and turned her head away from him. "Let me go! Why do you do this to me?"

He caught her hand and laughed. "Husbands and wives are supposed to do this. You and me haven't had much practice. We will though." He kissed the back of her hand. "You can count on it!"

She pulled free and brushed her hair out of her face. "I'll go change and we can leave."

"I'll saddle the horses. Pete and Repete can stay home and guard the place." Hadley reached for Maple again, but she jumped away. He laughed as she ran toward the house. "You won't always get away from me. You won't even want to!"

Her cheeks flamed as she ran inside the house. For one wild minute she'd wanted to stay in his arms. Why had he ruined it all by saying he loved her when it couldn't be true?

Taking a deep, steadying breath, she changed into her levis and shirt, then pulled on her boots with Breeches mewing around her ankles. "I'll be gone for a while, Breeches." She scratched the kitten behind the ears, grabbed her hat off the peg near the door, took another deep breath, and walked out to meet Hadley.

Just as they returned from the Smith's that evening, Rand rode in from visiting with Lucy. His
face shone with excitement. He turned his horse
into the corral just as Hadley and Maple did.

"You two are the first to know! Lucy and I are
gettin' hitched!"

Maple laughed while Hadley slapped Rand on
the back. "Tell me how it all came about," Maple
said as they leaned against the corral with Pete and
Repete at Hadley's feet.

Grinning from ear to ear, Rand pulled off his hat.
"I love that little gal and she loves me. She was
afraid she'd be stuck movin' from ranch to ranch
with me cowboyin' so I told her I'm an artist first
and foremost. She didn't believe me until I showed
her a picture Buck Lincoln bought from me a while
back. It's hangin' in his den right over his fireplace." Rand chuckled again. "She couldn't believe
it."

"When's the weddin' day?" Hadley asked, shaking Rand's hand.

"Next month."

"Poor Ed Turner. He's gonna drive out here one of
these days and he's gonna find Lucy married." Maple
giggled.

Rand cleared his throat and his eyes sparkled.
"You know the day I went to get my wagon from
Keene?"

"Sure," Hadley said.

"What'd you do?" Maple asked sharply. She saw
the mischief in Rand's face and knew it was going to
be a good story.

Rand leaned back against the fence and crossed his arms. "I paid a visit to that banker man. First he wouldn't see me, but when I said it had to do with Lucy Everett, he suddenly found time for me. I sat myself down in a chair across from him. He was perched behind his desk like a real important man with his white collar and slicked-back hair."

Maple laughed. "Tell the story, Rand."

"I told Ed Turner that me and Lucy were fallin' head over heels in love. He sputtered and spit, but I said it wouldn't do no good for him to pay a call on her. I said I was gonna marry her and he better keep his attention on some lady that wasn't spoke for."

"Where will you two live?" Hadley asked.

"At Buck Lincoln's. He don't want to lose Lucy as his housekeeper, so he said we could take the whole top floor of the house as ours. He says he knows people all over who would want my art. He says it reminds him of the good ole days when men were men and nobody had heard of barbed wire or homesteaders."

"When will you leave us?" Maple asked, feeling sad to think of his leaving.

"Just as soon as I finish helpin' train Buck's horses."

"My brothers helped me, so it won't take much more time." Hadley watched the horses swishing flies off their backs with their long tails. "They're first rate horseflesh, Rand."

"Buck's known for 'em. And with you trainin' for him, they'll bring top dollar. Buck knows it as well as I do."

"I was thinkin' with the money I make I should add on to the house." Hadley looked toward the house. He felt Maple stiffen beside him, but he didn't turn toward her. "It's never too early to plan for a family."

"I could help you build," Rand said. "I know some about buildin'."

"You know some about everything," Maple snapped. She strode away from them with her head high. Why was Hadley pushing her so hard? And now Rand was helping him. Next, Lucy would be in on it.

"Don't count on me for supper, Maple," Rand called after Maple. "I ate early with Lucy."

Maple closed the screen door with a snap. Breeches ran to her and she picked him up and held him close. He smelled of dust. "Breeches, how will it be to have Rand and Lucy happily married and living close enough to visit?" Breeches purred. Lucy and Rand had chosen to marry each other. It wasn't like with her and Hadley. They had been forced to marry and forced to stay together.

If she could choose now, would she stay with Hadley?

The question hit her hard and she set Breeches on the floor and gripped the back of a kitchen chair. Would she stay?

Impatiently she brushed the question aside. Why even think that way? She had no choice. This was her home and Hadley was her husband.

Breeches mewed at the door and Maple let him out. "Don't get in a fight with the dogs."

Maple banged the lid off the stove and started the fire. Soon she had cornbread in the oven and chicken and dumplings on the stove. Just as she was ready to call Hadley, he came in with the milk, strained it, and took it out to the well. He came back in, damp from washing at the well.

"Smells good in here," he said as he sat at the table.

"It seems empty with just the two of us." She folded her hands in her lap.

"Sure does." He smiled at her. "You pray, will you?"

She bowed her head and asked the blessing on the food. She wanted to pray for his family and even for Rand and Lucy, but she couldn't get the words out. She felt a strange tension from Hadley and she wondered if he was upset about Lucy marrying Rand. Or maybe he just missed his family.

Hadley ate in silence, often smiling at her.

"Elly asked if I'd help her can beef next week and I said I would."

"That's good." Hadley buttered a slice of cornbread. The butter melted down into the coarse yellow bread. "We'll make a day of it. I'll work with Obid while you help Elly."

Maple pushed a fluffy white dumpling around with her spoon. "Do you know when we can visit Momma and Papa?"

"Before snow flies."

"Maybe they'll come see us. They said they would."

Hadley nodded.

Maple locked her icy hands in her lap. "Why are you so quiet tonight?"

"I've been tryin' to find a way to tell you we're sharin' the bed tonight. I reckon it's best to just say it."

Maple turned hot all over. Helplessly she shook her head.

Slowly Hadley walked around the table and lifted her to her feet. "You're my wife and I love you. I think you love me too. Look in your heart."

She shook her head, her eyes wide with fear.

He took her in his arms and kissed her, softly, gently, then with a building passion.

Something melted on the inside of her, leaving her weak with a longing she couldn't understand. With a moan she slipped her arms around his neck and pushed her fingers in the soft thickness of his hair. She returned his kisses with a passion that matched his own.

CHAPTER 11

Maple stood in the yard between Buck and Hadley and waved to Lucy and Rand as they drove out of Buck's yard. Lucy's wedding had been small, but beautiful. Pastor VanArsdale had come from Keene to perform the short ceremony, and had left right afterwards. Hot August wind pressed Maple's light blue muslin dress against her long legs as she glanced at Hadley, then frowned slightly. What was he thinking that made him look so upset? Was he sorry to lose Lucy? Maple wanted to slip her hand in Hadley's arm, but she stood stiffly beside him. He had kept her at arm's length since the ceremony.

"Stay with me a while, you two," Buck said as he pushed his hat to the back of his head. "I feel like I lost my daughter."

"I have to do chores," Hadley said, his voice low and tight. "Comin', Maple?"

"No, I'll stay with Buck for a while."

A chill ran down Hadley's spine. He had listened to the wedding vows spoken between Lucy and Rand and it had brought back memories of his wedding. They had been forced to speak the vows. *Maple* had been forced to! One of these days she would realize she wasn't really bound to him and she'd ride away. She hadn't wanted to marry him, nor live with him, nor be a true wife to him. He'd forced her to stay. She never said she loved him and wanted to stay with him. Was she planning to leave him now? Buck would do anything for her, even help her leave him. Hadley nodded to them and walked to the corral to get Champion. He rode away without waving to Maple or Buck.

"I don't want you ridin' back alone," Buck said as they walked to the house. "Brenner will ride with you."

"I'm a big girl, Buck. I can go alone."

Buck squeezed her hand. "Brenner will ride with you. That's that."

"All right!" Maple laughed. "Shall we have more wedding cake?"

"Sounds good to me."

Later Maple changed into her levis and shirt and rode away from Buck's place with Brenner. She left him on the prairie in full view of the Rocking H and rode into the ranch yard at a gallop, expecting to see Hadley hard at work doing night chores. Suddenly she couldn't stand being away from him. She wanted to fling her arms around him and make the wedding vows real. Hearing Lucy and Rand exchange vows had made her realize she wanted to pledge herself to Hadley in that same manner—of her own free will.

She slid off Twister just as Pete and Repete ran to meet her. With the reins in hand she walked to the corral. "Boys, where's Hadley?" They swung their tails and whined. Frowning, she looked around. It was almost dark and Hadley should've been home. Had something happened to him? She unsaddled Twister, opened the gate, slapped him on the rump, and watched him race to the tank to drink. With cold water dribbling from his mouth Twister raced around the corral, stopped, and awkwardly rolled over.

Maple ran to the pump and splashed cold water over her face and rubbed it dry with the tail of her shirt. "Hadley!" she called. There was no answer. "Where on earth are you, Hadley?" She knew he had been home because the cow was milked, but what would take him away again? Had Obid needed him?

In the house Maple stripped off her hot levis and washed quickly, then dressed carefully in a yellow and brown calico that Lucy had made for her. With quick, hard strokes she brushed her tangled hair, twisted it in a knot, and pinned it at the nape of her neck. Darkness fell but she didn't light the lamp. With Breeches curled up in her lap and purring loudly, Maple waited in the rocker for the sound of hoofbeats. Where was Hadley? Her high-keyed excitement oozed away as the minutes ticked by. Had something happened to him?

With a sigh she leaned her head back and dozed. Crickets chirped and a night bird called. She was awakened by a sound. She sat still, barely breathing. The door opened and she saw Hadley silhouetted in the doorway. She started to speak, but no sound came out.

Hadley closed the door. "Maple, Maple, how can I live without you?" he whispered in anguish.

Tears sprang to her eyes. "Hadley?"

"Maple!" He struck a match and lit the lamp, then stared at her in shock. "There was no light. I thought you'd be gone!"

"What are you talkin about?"

"I was afraid you'd had enough of me and this place. I thought you wanted to leave and that Buck Lincoln was helpin' you." Hadley's voice broke. "I was goin' crazy with all those thoughts."

"I did think about leaving once—a long time ago. But I couldn't go."

He pulled her close and buried his face against her hair. "Thank God! You're my life, my dream come true. I can't live without you!"

She smiled as she wrapped her arms around him. He smelled of sweat and leather. "I have something to tell you."

"Not yet. I want to hold you, feel you against me. I know this is a dream, you comin' to me so willin'-like and I don't want it to end." He tipped up her face. "If I kiss you, will you disappear?"

"It's not a dream." She ran a finger over his lips. "I won't disappear."

He rubbed his hands over her and trembled. "You are real!"

She shivered with delight. She pulled his head down and covered his face with butterfly-light kisses. "I'm here to stay forever. As your . . . loving wife."

He covered her lips with his, then lifted her

easily and carried her to the bedroom.

The next morning she awoke to find him gone. She touched his pillow and smiled dreamily.

Maple washed and dressed in the yellow and brown calico that lay in a heap on the floor. Humming softly she made coffee and set it on the hot stove. What would she say to him when he walked in for breakfast? She blushed and felt shy again.

The screen door squawked as Hadley walked in, his hands behind his back. He smiled. "Good mornin', darlin'."

"Good morning." He looked so ordinary in his blue plaid shirt and faded levis that her shyness vanished and she smiled. "Breakfast will be ready soon."

"I have a surprise for you." Grinning, he walked slowly toward her.

"What is it?" She tried to peek around him, but he moved each time.

"Guess first."

"I don't know!"

"You'll like it."

"Hadd!"

He leaned down to her. "Give me a kiss first."

Her pulse leaped and she kissed him.

Slowly he slipped his hands around in front. Nestled in an open palm was a furry black kitten with four white legs and a white tail.

"Oh, Hadley, that's Breeches!" She took the kitten and rubbed her cheek against it.

Hadley chuckled. "I thought it'd be worth a first rate kiss."

"Don't ever think you have to buy my kisses," she whispered.

Hadley wrapped his arms around her and kissed her deeply. "I'm glad you didn't leave yesterday."

"Me too."

"We're truly married, Maple. Are you sorry?"

"No," she whispered. She kissed him again, then set Breeches behind the stove with a bowl of milk.

"I wish I didn't have to leave this morning." Hadley washed his face and hands. "But I told Obid I'd help him today."

"I have a lot to do anyway."

Hadley sighed. "I wish I could take you on a long honeymoon. Maybe next year I can get Tad to take care of our place and we can go somewhere."

"Maybe. But I don't even care, Hadley. You're my husband even if we never go on a honeymoon."

"You got that right, Red!" Hadley laughed as he tugged a stray strand of hair. "Did I ever tell you I always dreamed of havin' a red-haired wife?"

"Did you really?"

He nodded. "Dreams come true, don't they?" His eyes twinkled as he sat at the table.

Maple laughed and kissed him.

Midmorning Maple swept the kitchen floor and wished she'd gone with Hadley. It was lonely without him. Talking to Breeches wasn't quite the same as talking with Hadley.

A horse whinnied and another answered. Someone was coming! Maple ran outdoors. A buggy pulled by two black horses was coming toward her. She narrowed her eyes, then laughed excitedly. It was Momma and Papa! She ran to meet them, her skirts held high. Hot wind whirled the windmill and tugged at her hair.

Ben stopped the buggy near the barn and leaped down to pull her close. "I missed you terrible, daughter," he whispered.

"I didn't think we'd ever find this place," Leona said as she slowly climbed from the buggy. She brushed dust from her gray dress and straightened her bonnet. "We left at the crack of dawn and only stopped twice to water the horses."

Maple's heart sank. "Hello, Momma." She had almost forgotten what Momma was like.

Leona gazed all around, then studied the house. "How can you live in such a tiny house, Maple?"

"It's big enough for me and Hadd."

"Now, Leona, we had a small house in the beginning."

Leona scowled at Ben. "I want Maple to have better than we did!"

"Don't you worry about her. She looks mighty happy and contented to me."

"I am," Maple whispered.

"Nonsense! How can you be happy when you have to work so hard and live in a house no bigger than a cheese box?"

"Where's Hadley?" Ben asked.

"Helping Obid Smith, our neighbor." Maple's muscles tightened and she felt a headache starting.

Inside the house Leona looked around with a frown. Breeches walked from behind the stove and wove around Maple's ankle.

"A cat in the house?" Leona cried, her round face red. "Get it out right now!"

"Now, Leona, this is Maple's house." Ben poured himself a cup of coffee. "Let the cat be."

Maple bit her lip, then slowly picked up Breeches and put him outdoors. He ran across the yard to the barn. It wasn't worth a fight. When Momma left, Breeches could come back.

Maple poured Momma a cup of coffee and they sat at the table. Maple's stomach fluttered nervously.

"Ed Turner got himself a bride. Married yesterday," Leona said sharply. "To a stranger. You should have been his wife, Maple."

"Now, Leona."

Maple locked her hands in her lap. "Momma, I'm happy with Hadley."

"No one knows how Mr. Turner met the woman or how long they knew each other. I tried to learn all the details, but Mr. Turner was close-mouthed about it all. Her name is Barbara and she came from Omaha."

Maple hid a smile. She would never tell Momma Hadley was a better husband than Ed could ever be.

"I reckon Hadley will be startin' fall round-up soon," Ben said.

Maple nodded. She intended to help, but she didn't say so.

"We brought you some things." Leona stood and brushed her hands down her gray dress. "I didn't know if you'd have enough dishes or silver or bed linens. I canned green beans for you and some corn too. Papa brought a couple of hams and ten pounds of bacon."

"Thank you." Maple wanted to tell them Hadley was a good provider, but she accepted everything graciously and found a place to store it all.

Leona walked to the far side of the kitchen and frowned. "I think I'd like the table under the window, Maple. Help me move it, will you?"

Maple's temper flared. "Momma, I like the table in the middle of the room."

"I don't!"

"Now, Leona. This is Maple's house." Ben patted Leona and smiled.

Leona jerked away. "I only wanted to help."

Maple looked around the room and suddenly realized just how tiny it was. Maybe the table would be better under the window.

Just then Hadley walked in with Breeches in his hand. He stopped short when he saw Leona and Ben. "I wondered who was here. Nice to see you both." He set Breeches on the floor and shook hands, then stepped to Maple's side. He started to slip his arm around her, but she moved away. He lifted his brow inquiringly.

She picked up Breeches. "Supper will be ready soon."

Leona grabbed the kitten from Maple. "That cat does not belong in the house!"

Hadley reached out and took the kitten from Leona. "He stays in here. He's Maple's pet."

"Cats belong in the barn!"

Maple touched Hadley's arm and begged him with her eyes to let it drop. With a shrug he put

Breeches outdoors and walked to the washstand and washed his hands and face.

Later Hadley took Ben and Leona for a tour around the place. Maple hung back but Hadley caught her hand and held her beside him as he talked about how well the rose bushes were doing and when the fruit trees would bear. They walked to the corral and looked at the horses. Hadley slipped his arm around Maple and she tried to pull away. He tightened his hold and whispered, "We're married. Relax."

She smiled stiffly.

He kissed her, his lips barely touching hers. "I love you."

His words warmed her, but her muscles tightened at the thought of Momma seeing them embrace.

At the supper table Ben said, "Maple tells us you were helpin' Obid Smith today."

Hadley nodded. "He has a boy, but sometimes needs a man to help him."

"I always wanted a boy," Ben said.

Maple froze. She'd heard that all her life. Why couldn't he be pleased with her?

"We plan on having at least five boys and three girls," Hadley said, winking at Maple.

Leona gasped.

Maple flushed scarlet.

"And I want 'em all red-headed and beautiful like their ma."

"Tell them our plans, Ben," Leona said impatiently.

Maple bit back an anguished cry.

Ben cleared his throat and pushed his chair back from the table. "We'd like you children to live near us. There's a place for sale and I thought of buyin' it for a wedding gift for you two."

Hadley leaned back in his chair. "That's a mighty generous offer, Ben."

"It's yours then," Leona said, looking pleased. "I knew you wouldn't pass it up."

Maple stared at Hadley. Was he going to accept it?

Hadley shook his head. "We can't take it though." He waved his hand in an arc. "This is our home. We've worked hard and it's ours. We fought for it and won. How about you save that ranch for one of your grandchildren?"

Her face brick-red, Leona scraped back her chair and jumped up. Her breast rose and fell in agitation. "Talk some sense into him, Ben!"

Maple longed for the floor to swallow her.

"I wasn't goin' to take no for an answer, my boy, but I know how you feel. You keep this place. We will think about giving the other to a grandson."

"Grandson indeed!" Leona sank to the rocker and brushed tears from her eyes. "We might not even be around by then."

"Sure you will," Hadley said, grinning.

Maple jumped up and started to clear off the table. She didn't want to talk about having children in front of Momma and Papa.

"Let me wash the dishes," Leona said, lifting the heavy teakettle. "I do a better job than you."

Maple stepped aside and let Momma take over

just as she always had in the past. She felt Hadley's look, but she wouldn't meet his gaze.

After dark Leona yawned and said, "I'd like to go to bed, Maple. I've decided you and me will share the bed and the men can sleep in the barn."

Maple shot a look at Hadley.

Hadley slipped an arm around Maple. "We'll sleep in the sod house. You and Ben take our bed."

"I will not allow a daughter of mine to sleep in a sod house. Of all things!"

Maple saw the stubborn set of Momma's chin and knew she must give in or have a terrible fight on her hands. She slipped away from Hadley. "I'll sleep in here. You take plenty of bedding out for you and Papa."

Hadley's jaw tightened. He studied Maple thoughtfully, then without a word he gathered up a pile of bedding and walked out with Ben close behind him.

Maple's heart sank. What did he want her to do? He knew she couldn't stand against Momma!

Two days later Maple stood in the yard with the stars twinkling overhead and Pete and Repete at her feet. Soon she'd have to go in and climb into bed with Momma. Tears pricked Maple's eyes, but she wouldn't let them fall. Momma would be gone in two days and then life would be normal and happy again.

But would it? Maple bit her lip. For two days Hadley hadn't touched her, kissed her, or talked to her unless it was necessary. He was hurt because she ignored him and wouldn't take his side against

Momma when she criticized him. Maple wiped a tear off her cheek. She didn't blame Hadley for being upset.

Slowly Maple walked to the corral and leaned against the fence. Horses milled around. In the distance a coyote yapped. Papa was inside the house with Momma. Hadley was somewhere outdoors, but she couldn't call to him in case he wouldn't answer. She couldn't stand to have him reject her.

Pete whined and wagged his tail. Repete copied him. Maple turned. Hadley was walking toward her, his head bare, and his shirt hanging down over his levis. He leaned against the corral fence and looked at her. Her heart stood still.

"I'm sorry for gettin' hurt and mad and ignorin' you, darlin'."

"Oh, Hadd! I'm the one who's sorry!"

He pulled her close and held her, his heart thudding against hers. "Maple, you're a woman. You can chose how to live your life. Your momma can't make you do anything."

"She gets me so upset!"

Hadley looked into Maple's face. "Do you love me?"

She trembled. She loved him with a wild, passionate love that consumed her. Why hadn't she told him?

"Do you?"

She wanted to answer him, but he looked too stern and seemed too far away and she couldn't force out the words.

He sighed raggedly and let her go. "I thought

you did. I reckon I was wrong."

"Don't . . . Just wait until they're gone."

"You're a woman, Maple. You won't accept yourself as one until your momma knows you're one. Go tell her."

Maple leaned weakly against the fence. "I just can't!"

"Yes, you can. I know you can if you try. You're brave, Maple. You're full of courage. I know just how bold and daring you are. God will help you." He cupped her face between his hands and kissed her slowly and deeply.

She moaned and leaned against him, wrapping her arms around him. He smelled so familiar!

The door slammed and Ben called out, "Maple, your momma's askin' for you."

Maple sprang away from Hadley. "Tell her I'll be right there."

"You belong with me," Hadley whispered hoarsely.

She ducked her head and sighed raggedly.

Hadley turned and strode to the sod house and disappeared inside.

Maple walked slowly toward the house. She stopped beside Papa.

"What is it, daughter?"

"I want to be with Hadley. He is my husband."

"Then stay in the sod house with him. I'll stay inside with your momma."

"She'll get mad at me!"

Ben lifted Maple's chin with his fingers. "She'll get over it."

"I'm afraid."

"I have something to tell you." Ben walked her to the bench and sat with her. "The day you and Hadley were married I rode out after you. I could have brought you home that day, but I didn't. I knew I'd rather have you married to Hadd Clements any day than Ed Turner."

"Papa!"

"Your momma doesn't know."

"Oh, Papa!"

"I brought her here to show her you're better off. But you're the one who has to convince her. She wants you to be happy."

"Then why doesn't she let me be?"

"She is who she is. But if you talked to her and made her understand, she would."

Maple shivered. "I don't know if I can talk to her."

"You can."

"Then I will!" Silently she asked the Lord to help her. "Give me a few minutes, then you come inside."

"That's my girl!" Ben patted Maple's back. "I'm proud of you, Maple."

"Even though you always wanted a son?"

"Sure! I have the best daughter in the world, but that don't make me stop wishin' for a son."

Maple smiled. Papa loved her! She didn't have to prove anything to him! She hugged him tight. "I love you!"

"I love you, daughter."

With a low laugh Maple ran to the house and

right into the bedroom. She took a deep breath. "Momma, I have to tell you something important."

"Make it short. I'm almost asleep."

"Momma, I love Hadley." Oh, she did love him! She loved him more than she ever thought she could love someone! "And I intend to sleep in the sod house with him. I want to live my own life the way I want to live it. And Momma, I will even keep Breeches in the house!"

Leona gasped, then burst into tears.

"Don't cry, Momma. I am a woman. But I'm still your daughter. I want to love you and I want you to love me."

"Why are you doing this?" Leona sobbed harder, the quilt tight to her chin. Her white nightcap covered her hair.

Maple fingered the cuff of her dress as she stood close to the bed. "When you married Papa did Grandma Raines try to run your life?"

Leona sat bolt upright. "Yes! Yes, she did!"

"Did you want her to? Did you let her?"

Leona slowly shook her head. "But it's not the same, Maple. I don't want you to make any mistakes. I don't want you to be sad."

"I'm happy with Hadley. I love him." The words rolled off her tongue as if she was used to saying them. Yet, she had never been able to say them aloud to Hadley. "I like working the ranch with him."

Leona studied Maple for a long time, then nodded. "I see you do. You run along and let me get some sleep. Send your papa in here so he can get his rest."

Maple touched Momma's soft cheek. "I love you."

"I love you. Now, let me get some sleep." Leona laid back down and pulled the covers to her chin.

Maple grabbed her nightdress and ran outdoors. "Papa, go on in. We'll see you in the morning."

Ben hugged her close, then hurried inside.

Maple took a deep, steadying breath and ran to the sod house. The lantern on the small table in the middle of the room cast a soft glow over Hadley. He sat on the bed against the sod wall, one leg up with his knee almost touching his chin. His boots stood beside him. He looked sad and lonely. She stepped into the light. Slowly he stood. Her throat closed over and blood roared in her ears.

"I'm afraid I'm dreamin," he said softly. "If I touch you, will you disappear?"

She dropped her nightclothes on the bed. "No. I'm here to stay."

"Are you sure?"

She nodded. "I love you, Hadley Clements."

Tears glistened in his dark eyes. "Say it again. Please."

"I love you," she whispered.

"I waited so long to hear that!" He held out his arms and she stepped into them.

"I was going to change into my levis and shirt to come out here, but I didn't want to take the time."

"I'm glad you didn't. I was beginning to think I'd have to put those things in the trunk with the blue gingham dress."

Maple drew back. That terrible dress! Why was

he bringing it up now of all times?

"What's wrong?"

"I hate that dress."

"You do? Then you won't ever have to wear it."

She frowned. "I don't understand you. You wouldn't *let* me wear it."

He trailed his fingers down her cheek. "Last winter a peddler came by with that dress and I was feelin' so lonely I bought it to give to my wife. All winter I'd look at that dress and dream about my wife wearin' it."

"But you got so angry when I had it on."

He ran his thumb over her bottom lip. "When I saw you standin' in my house at my stove, at my table, with that dress on, I wanted you to stay forever as my wife. I wanted it so bad I ached inside. All you wanted was to get out of there and back to town to that banker man." Hadley groaned. "I couldn't stand to see you with that dress on when I knew you wanted to be another man's wife."

"I only want to be your wife. Forever!" She kissed him, then pulled away. "Tomorrow I'll dress in the blue gingham and stand at your table and cook at your stove. I will mend your socks and wash your clothes."

He shook his head and laughed. "Tomorrow you'll wear your levis and shirt no matter what your momma says and ride with me to round up the mares we're sellin' to John Parkins."

Maple slid her arms around Hadley's neck and laughed softly. "Anything you say."

"It's what we both say." Hadley smiled into her

eyes, then touched his lips to hers in a kiss she returned   gladly.